TRADERS IN TIME

A Dream-Quest Adventure

Janie Lynn Panagopoulos

River Road Publications, Inc.
Spring Lake, Michigan

ISBN: 0-938682-24-5 (hardcover)

ISBN: 0-938682-27-X (paperback)

Printed in the United States of America

Copyright © 1993 by Janie Lynn Panagopoulos
All rights reserved. No part of this book may be reproduced or
utilized in any form or by any means, electronic or mecha--
nical, including photocopying, recording or by an information
storage and retrieval system, without permission in writing
from the publisher. Inquiries should be addressed to River
Road Publications, Inc., 830 East Savidge Street, Spring Lake,
MI 49456.

For my mother, Betty Blount, who nurtured my love for history and was always encouraging, and Kristi Karis, a true friend who supported me in all my efforts.

Contents

Author's Forward

The story contained in this book is called documentary fiction. It is a story based upon research and the interpretation of the life of Medelaine La Fromboise (also Madelaine and Magdelaine), a female fur trader who lived between 1780 and 1846 in western Michigan. Liberty has been taken with the facts of her life to create a lively fictional story about the history of the fur trade in the western Great Lakes region. Yet much of the drama comes from the human epic, the adventure, the hopes and defeats that surrounded the lives of the people who lived here at the time.

The job of the historian is to keep alive the human element of history. Guided by research and inspired by memories and sentiment, historians attempt to give their writing a spark of life blended with documented facts. Spending time in research is essential to the competent writer of history, since the task of weaving a story to include these facts is often difficult. It is my hope that this story will serve as an enduring testament to the lives and adventures of the people who worked in the region's early fur trade.

Chapter 1
Grand Haven

"I'm going to the top of the dune," Chris called to his brother. "I want to climb the old Indian tree in the center of the woods. Hurry up, let's go!"

Nicholas, Chris's eight-year-old brother paused for a moment. His freckled face and blue eyes showed disapproval. "Mom said not to climb that old tree again— and not to go into the woods alone!"

"Mom says, Mom says. Is that all you think about, Nick?" Chris snapped. "I never saw an eight-year-old wimp like you before." Christopher's blue eyes sparkled, knowing he was making his brother cross by teasing him.

"I'm not a wimp, and if you don't cut it out I'll—I'll— "

"What? Go tell Mom?" Chris laughed. "You'll have to wait until she gets back from the store. Christopher turned and climbed farther up the giant hill of sand, his bare feet sinking deep with each step.

"I wish I could be canoeing on the big lake right now," Chris thought to himself. "I bet the water is nice and cool out there."

A playful June breeze blew across Lake Michigan, swirling the sand around Nicholas's feet as he stood on the beach below the dune. Nick watched as his big brother, twelve-year-old Christopher, climbed the sand dune. Chris's long chestnut hair blew around his face and his red canteen swung from side to side across his back with each step he took.

"Hey, Chris," Nick called up to his brother. "You look really funny. Your hair is blowing all over the place."

"No kidding. A mountain man can't climb a mountain and not get his hair a mess, just like a wimp can't climb a sand dune without getting sand in his shoes." Chris turned suddenly, kicking sand at Nicholas with his bare feet. "Come on, I'm going to the top."

"Wait! I'd better take my shoes off, too."

"Okay, Wimp, I'll see you up there."

"I'm not a wimp," Nick thought, as he sat on the cool beach and pulled his tennis shoes off. A cascade of sand poured from each one. Putting the laces together, Nicholas tied his shoestrings through his belt loop, leaving the shoes dangling loosely at his side.

Nick could see Chris already sitting at the top of the sand dune in the shade of an old dead pine tree. The pine stuck out from the side of the dune, casting odd shadows in the sand. Chris buried his legs up to his knees in the sand and sat back enjoying the shade. "You know Chrissy," jeered Nick, "Mom's going to be real mad when she finds out you came to the beach again without your shoes."

"Well, how is she going to know unless someone tells on me again? Anyway, my feet are tough. I can handle it. I don't need to wear shoes all the time like some wimps I know."

"I'm not a wimp," Nick repeated to himself as he started up the dune toward Christopher.

The sand along the beach where Nicholas had been standing was cool. The waves from the lake licked up along the shoreline, bathing it in cool foam. Here on the dune, however, where only the hot sun and the wind could reach, the sand was hot—like burning coals.

"Ouch! The sand's on fire!" Nick yelled, hopping from one foot to the other.

"Hurry up, it's cooler up here," Chris yelled. "If you don't run all the way up, you'll burn your feet even more."

Nick hopped from one foot to the other all the way up the hot hill of sand, where Chris sat drinking from his red canteen. Teasingly, Chris sloshed water back and forth in his mouth, blowing tall spouts of water high into the air.

"Are you hot, Nicky?" Chris jeered. "Would you like a nice drink of water?"

Nicholas, reaching the top of the dune, sat in the shade beside Chris and fanned his feet. The sand there beside the tree was cooler. Nick lay back in the shadows of the gnarled pine. The hot Michigan sun burned in the sky above like a white fireball, making Nicholas see red dots every time he blinked his eyes.

"You want a drink ?" Chris asked again.

"No thanks. I'm not a wimp, are you?" Nick squinted a grin at his brother.

"You know," said Chris ignoring his brother's comment, "I should have brought Dad's binoculars with me. I bet I could see all the way across Lake Michigan to Wisconsin." Chris stood, catching his balance in the sand hole and dusting off his jeans.

Nick jumped up from the sand and swung his body onto the weathered trunk of the dead pine. For a moment he imagined himself at the bow of an old sailing vessel. "Dad wouldn't let you use the binoculars 'cause you're always losing things. And anyway, you couldn't see across Lake Michigan. It's ninety miles across there to Wisconsin."

"OK, genius," Chris sneered, "but I'd still like to see Wisconsin. I've heard it looks a lot like Michigan, with all the trees and water and stuff. I wish I could get out on the big lake and canoe over there today. Wouldn't it be fun, Nick? Hey, maybe we could make a dugout canoe from this dead tree and go for a paddle to Wisconsin. What do you think?"

"Yeah, we'd be like voyageurs," said Nick. "Or maybe hunters, like some of the Indians, selling our furs to traders in Wisconsin or even at Mackinac Island.

"Yeah, that'd be fun," said Chris and smiled at his brother.

This was Chris's favorite time of the year. School was out and he could spend the whole summer exploring the woods and beach around his home in the small Michigan city of Grand Haven. The best part of Grand Haven, Chris thought, was its location along the shore of Lake Michigan, one of the Great Lakes. Once, a long time ago, the Odawa (A-da-wa) and Potawatomi (Pot-a-wa-toe-me) Indians lived in the area. They called Grand Haven *Gabagouache* (Gab-a-go-wa-che), or "big mouth," because there the wide mouth of the Grand River opened to join Lake Michigan.

Summer after summer, for as long as Chris could remember, he and Nick had explored the beach, dunes, and woods near their home. Chris was always the explorer, and Nick always followed. One of Chris's favorite spots was an old tree that stood in the middle of the woods beyond the top of the dunes. It was the tallest tree in the whole forest and was hundreds of years old. Large rocks surrounded the tree, and Chris and his friends liked to believe that something special had happened here long ago. The tree must have been just a sapling then, Chris had decided. Now it was a giant.

"Let's go to the old tree," Chris said. "I want to climb it again. Maybe this time, I'll be able to reach the top and see the lake from up there."

Nick, remembering the last time Chris tried climbing the old tree, cringed at the idea. "Mom will be mad. Last time you climbed that tree, you got that sticky stuff all over you."

"That sticky stuff is pine pitch, Nick. The Indians and traders were smart enough to use it to keep mosquitoes away. I don't know why Mom got mad. It's only a natural bug repellent.

"Come on, you're not going to back out on me now are you?" Chris begged. "Let's race to the tree. You'll win this time 'cause you can put your shoes back on and I'll be barefoot."

Nick thought for a moment and jumped down from the trunk of the tree. Quickly he untied his shoe laces from his belt loop. "OK, I'll race you."

Chris pulled his feet from the sand hole and both boys ran to the crest of the dune. There the windblown sand from the dune mixed with the shadows from the woods, making the earth dark and cool.

Standing on a soft cushion of pine needles, the boys turned and looked out over Lake Michigan. From that height, they could see for miles. The water glistened and danced like a thousand tiny sun diamonds. "I sure would like to be out there canoeing today," said Chris.

"Yeah, me too." Nick smiled and sat down in the pine needles to put on his shoes. He could smell the soft, sweet smell of pine from the woods. He liked the woods as much as Christopher liked the lake. Struggling with his shoes, Nick tried to force them on without untying his laces. Jumping up and down he pushed hard with the toe of his shoe into a lump of hard sand.

"Ouch, that hurts! I hit something!"

Chris laughed as he watched Nick dig into a ball of sunbaked sand. "Don't be a wimp, Nick."

"I'm not, Chris, but that hurt! Hey! I think I found something in the sand. It's a rock."

"Oh no, you don't," said Chris shaking his head. "No more rocks."

"Yeah, but Chris, it looks like a turtle warrior. Yeah, that's it. You can see its arms and legs."

Chris leaned over to take a closer look at the rock. Investigating all the angles, he shook his head in disapproval. "Nick, it's just another stupid rock. Put it down and let's get going."

Nick was sure Chris hadn't really looked closely and shoved the rock into his face.

"Here, it even looks like it has a shell." Licking his finger, Nick ran it across the rock, leaving a wet stain. "Look, it's shiny underneath."

"You're gross. Get it out of my face!" Chris pulled back and pushed Nick's hand away. "Nick, it's a rock. You have tons of them at home, and you're always leaving them lying around for me to step on. Just put it back. I'm not carrying that thing. If you want it, you carry it."

Nick checked the rock over once again and was sure it was something special. He could add it to his rock collection, along with his dinosaur rock and his horse rock. These were all special rocks to Nick. They were magical, and now he had a magic turtle warrior rock. Nick smiled and slipped the rock into his pocket when Chris wasn't looking. What did Chris know about rocks, anyway?

The boys stopped and took one last look at the lake with its many shades of blue and its dancing white waves. Nick patted his pocket, making sure his rock was safe and they started toward the woods.

"You know, Chris, if we were traders we would have had a birchbark canoe, not a dugout. The Indians around here cut bark from birch trees and sewed it together to make canoes. They were light and easier to carry when they had to carry them across land."

"Where did you learn all this stuff, Nick? I think you spend too much time with Mom at the museum."

Nick smiled, because he knew Chris spent lots of time at the museum, too. That was where their mother worked. And besides, Chris always reminded Nick that he had been to the museum a zillion times more because he was older.

The trail that led through the woods was worn and scattered with pine needles and pine cones. "You sure you want to race barefoot on all these needles, Chris? I bet they'll feel like tiny arrows going into your feet."

"Nice try, Nick. You're just afraid I'll beat you to the tree, barefoot and all. Do you remember where the tree is?" Chris asked in a smart-alec voice.

"How could I forget, Chrissy? It's the biggest tree in the woods and has all those rocks around it."

"Those rocks," said Chris, "are there because they mark where something special happened a long time ago."

"Yeah right, Chris. So what happened there? You don't even know! I think you and your friends put those rocks there so you could find the tree again. You're always trying to trick me, Chris. I know you."

Chris shook his head at Nick. "Well, this is no trick. I'll beat you to the tree!" Chris took off running as fast as he could down the old path, swatting the low-hanging branches from his face as he ran.

Surprised that Chris had left, Nick thought, I'll show him. I'll take a shortcut through the woods and beat him by a mile. Nick raced into the woods away from the trail, scratching up against trees and running into bushes. The woods were dark and all Nicholas could see were silver diamonds dancing before his eyes where he had looked at the sun's reflection for too long.

Pushing forward, Nick could feel the branches scratching at his face and ripping at his clothes. Putting his arms in front of him, he ran even harder. All of a sudden—SWOOSH! A low tree branch pushed back against Nicholas's arms and threw him to the ground.

Nick lay there for a moment. Then, trying to sit up, he began to feel dizzy. He fell back again, grabbing handfuls of pine needles and hard sand beneath him. Nick held them as the woods spun in circles around him.

Chapter 2

Meggie

"*Bonjour*, little one. Are you all right?" a voice said in a whisper.

"I'm OK. I'm all right. I just fell." Nick opened his eyes and slowly sat up, rubbing his head. The woods had stopped spinning.

"Wow, I won't take that shortcut again." Looking around, Nick searched to find where the voice had come from.

There in front of him stood a very tall woman with long black braided hair, wearing the strangest dress he'd ever seen. It was decorated all over with beads and shells and ribbons.

"You sure you're all right, little English? My name is Medelaine La Framboise, but you may call me Meggie. I am a habitant here in these woods.

"I heard you running. I thought you were a great deer by the sound you were making. I was wanting the taste of venison for my soup. Now, I find you, just a fawn!" Meggie laughed out loud and offered Nicholas her hand to help him to his feet.

Nicholas did not find this woman funny at all. A little fawn, he thought, I'm not a little fawn.

"It's OK. I can get up by myself," Nicholas jeered.

"*Bon*, that is a good English fawn," said Meggie.

"I'm not English, I'm American!" Nicholas snapped before thinking about his manners.

Meggie stepped back a few paces and looked closely at Nicholas. Her dark eyes narrowed suspiciously.

"Whom are you with?" she asked. "You cannot be here alone in these woods, so far from the fort."

"My brother and I were out exploring. We were racing to the big tree in the middle of the woods when I fell," Nick explained.

"You, an explorer? Your brother is big, no?" She asked.

"He is too big, and he's real strong! He's got a red canteen and everything."

"I see," Meggie said. "Maybe you should come to my post, little American. I can give you cider to drink and then we find your brother and his red canteen."

Just then, Nicholas and Meggie heard sounds of someone walking through the underbrush.

"That's my big brother now. He's probably looking for me. I've got to go. I'm not supposed to talk to strangers."

Nicholas turned and ran into the woods toward the direction of the sound. What a strange woman, he thought. Now I know why Mom doesn't want us to play in the woods alone. Nick looked behind him to see if the woman was still watching. She had disappeared.

"Chris, Chris," Nick called. "I hear you. Where are you?" Nick stood silently trying to decide in which direction to go.

"Chris, if you're trying to hide from me this isn't funny. I gotta tell you something."

Just then, Nick turned and walked straight into the biggest mountain of a man he had ever seen. The man's skin was as black and shiny as one of his Obsidian rocks. His eyes were big and fierce. And from his ears dangled enormous gold earrings, and around his arm hung Chris's canteen.

The two stood there for a moment staring at each other. And then a big toothy grin came to the face of the giant. He reached out and grabbed hold of Nicholas by both arms.

"Hey, I'm gonna tell my brother. Let me go! That's his canteen. Where did you get that?" Nicholas fought, squirming under the steel grip of the man's large hands. Laughing loudly, the giant picked Nicholas up by both arms and lifted him high into the air. Struggling even more, Nicholas kicked his legs wildly as the giant carried him deep into the woods.

"Put me down! Put me down! What did you do with my brother?" Nick demanded.

Just then Nick heard a sharp voice call out. "LeClaire, put that American fawn down." It was the voice of the strange woman Nicholas had met in the woods. It was Meggie.

LeClaire stopped walking and lifted Nicholas high into the air until they were eye-to-eye. "You American?" the giant asked with the same accent as the woman.

"Yes, I'm American, and I'm not a fawn. My name is Nicholas Corey. And where did you get my brother's canteen?" Nick gave the giant the meanest look he had ever given anybody. The giant man laughed loudly and slowly lowered Nick to the ground.

"I am sorry little one, Nicholas," Meggie said as she made her way through the bush. "My partner LeClaire is very careful about strangers who come to visit our woods."

"Your woods! This land belongs to Grand Haven and the state of Michigan. He can't go around treating people like that!"

LeClaire stood silently and hung his head. Meggie spoke to LeClaire with words Nicholas could not understand. He did, however, hear his name and the word American.

"Where did you get my brother's canteen?" Nick insisted.

LeClaire looked strangely at Nicholas not understanding what he meant.

"The canteen, the canteen, this!" Nicholas reached out and pulled the red strap that hung around the giant's arm.

"This I find in the woods along the path. This can-teen?" LeClaire repeated the word as if he had never heard it before.

"That belongs to my brother and he is going to want it back."

Meggie motioned to LeClaire to give Nicholas the canteen.

LeClaire stooped low and placed the strap of the canteen around the boy's arm and smiled. "Pardon, Monsieur Nicholas," the giant spoke in a deep voice. "I apologize for making you afraid. It is not often people come to this place in the woods."

Satisfied, Nicholas reached out to shake hands with LeClaire. "Apology accepted," said Nick, grabbing LeClaire's huge hand with both of his. Meggie and LeClaire laughed, and Nicholas laughed too.

Meggie led the group to a nearby clearing where a small log cabin stood. "Welcome to my post," Meggie said in a gentle voice. "What I have, you are welcome to. LeClaire, my partner, is really a *le gentil geant* (gee-ant). A gentle giant as you Americans say. You have no reason to fear him."

"This looks like a nice place," said Nick," but I can't stay. I have to find my brother Christopher. I was supposed to race him to the big tree. Do you know which direction I could find the big tree? It's the biggest one in all the woods."

Meggie and LeClaire looked at each other and shook their heads. "*Non, mon ami* (No, my friend). I am sorry but all the trees are big in this woods." said Meggie.

LeClaire stooped down, looking at Nicholas face-to-face. "Why is it," LeClaire asked in a deep voice, "that you came to the woods? You are not an American spy, are you? Here to find how Madame La Framboise makes good trade with the Odawa?"

"LeClaire!" Meggie interrupted. "The boy said he and his brother were explorers. The tree he speaks of must be blazed for a new American trail through the forest."

Nicholas wrinkled his face and wondered what she meant.

"The tree is nothing special," said Nick. "Just a place where my brother and I go to play. It has great big rocks around it."

"Madame," said LeClaire, "I know of only one place surrounded by rocks of that size." Meggie and LeClaire stared down at Nicholas, giving him a look that made him feel uncomfortable.

Who are these people with strange accents? thought Nick. Maybe they are foreign spies who got lost in their submarine on the Great Lakes. They're probably hiding here until their friends pick them up. Nick remembered seeing a movie like that once.

LeClaire stood tall again and stretched his long legs. He was wearing short pants that tied at the knees. Meggie patted him on the arm. "It is fine, old friend," she said. "The boy is no spy. He does not even know where he is. I do not think he is even much of an explorer."

Nicholas resented that remark. He knew the woods as well as Christopher did, even though he had never seen this place before.

"Monsieur Nicholas," said Meggie, "you are welcome to rest. I will make you something to eat, if you like."

Nicholas thought he would rather go find Christopher. Just then he heard a strange buzzing, humming sound. He turned to find LeClaire with a funny looking piece of twisted metal held to his mouth.

"What's that?" Nick asked Meggie.

"That? Oh, that is LeClaire with his Jew's harp," said Meggie. "Go sit and listen to him. He plays many fine songs."

Nicholas moved closer to LeClaire, who was sitting on an old tree stump. His moccasined foot beat up and down on the hard sand.

"You like, Monsieur Nicholas?" LeClaire asked. "You try." LeClaire handed Nick the bent piece of metal. Nick pulled the red canteen from his arm and handed it to LeClaire.

"We no make trade, my friend," said LeClaire, who put the canteen down on the ground next to the stump.

"Put the harp to your mouth like this." LeClaire reached around Nicholas's head and placed the metal object to Nick's lips.

"Now make music. You know French *chansons*?" LeClaire asked.

"I know a song in French," Nicholas said. "I learned it in school. Hey, are you two French?"

Both Meggie and LeClaire smiled and nodded their heads at Nick.

"Madame is *Métis*, part French, part Indian. I am from Port Royal, and was once a French slave. Now I am a man of business."

Nicholas scrunched up his face and wondered what the giant meant. Port Royal. Nick had never heard of that place before. And a slave? The giant must be joking.

"You make music now, we talk later," said LeClaire. "Make the song in your mouth without words. Hold the harp up to your lips."

Nick frowned at LeClaire. "How do you make a song in your mouth without words?"

"You mean hum? You want me to hum?" Nick exclaimed.

LeClaire, shook his head yes, and pressed the Jew's harp against Nicholas's lips. Nick started to hum, "*Alouette, gentille alouette.*" LeClaire's eyes opened wide, and a great smile came to his mouth. "*Bon, bon,* it is good French *chanson.*"

Nick hummed across the harp and LeClaire began to twang a short piece of metal on the harp, snapping it across Nicholas's lips. The low, buzzing twang of the Jew's harp translated Nicholas's hum into a new sound.

"I can do it!" Nick said. He was as surprised as LeClaire with the sound he was making.

"Meggie, *comme c'est va*, come hear what the boy plays."

Meggie, who was in the cabin, came to the door. She watched and listened as Nicholas hummed and twanged the metal harp. LeClaire stomped his giant moccasined feet and clapped his hands to the music.

"You know *Alouette*?" Meggie said. "That song makes me hungry. How about you?"

Nick stopped playing, his lips tingling from the twang of the Jew's harp. "Is that about food?"

"You know *Alouette*, but you don't understand the words?" Meggie said. "LeClaire, tell the boy about the song."

LeClaire stood with all his greatness and sang a loud, booming version of *Alouette* to Nicholas in French. His voice was clear and fine, making Nicholas feel like the song had real meaning.

Then LeClaire paused for a moment and began to sing the song in English.

"Little lark, gentle little lark, little lark I will pluck you. First the head, *la tête*" LeClaire pointed to the red bandana on his head. "Then the beak, *le bec*," LeClaire puckered his mouth up and bobbed his head from side to side. "Then the nose, *le nez*," and he reached out and placed his big finger on Nicholas's nose and pushed hard. "Then the whole bird! When you done, *voilà!* You throw the bird in the soup pot!"

"Yuck, that's gross, LeClaire," said Nick. "Don't sing that anymore." LeClaire burst into laughter as Nicholas scrunched up his face.

"The tune's so nice. I thought it was about sailing on Lake Michigan."

"*Lac Michigand* is fine *lac*, no?" LeClaire asked.

"It's a fine lake, yes. It's beautiful. My brother and I want to go canoeing on it in a birchbark, all the way to Wisconsin."

"*Ouisconsin, non—Ile de Michilimackinac, Mackinac,* that is good." LeClaire's eyes gleamed as he bobbed his head up and down.

"Mackinac Island. My brother and I have been there lots of times with our Mom and Dad. It's neat. I wish Chris could meet you and Meggie. He'd like you both."

"I wonder where Chris is? I hope he's OK. When I find him, I'll bring him back to meet you and Meggie. He'll be glad you found his canteen." Nick looked at LeClaire and Meggie.

Meggie, standing in the door of the cabin, said to LeClaire, "Maybe you go with the little American to find his brother?"

LeClaire, seeing the concern in Meggie's face, said only one word, "McDougal?"

Meggie nodded yes.

"What's a McDougal?" Nicholas asked.

"It is not what, but who." Meggie responded.

"McDougal is *Le Diable Rouge*, the Red Devil," said LeClaire as he scowled and narrowed his eyes.

"He is not good, that one. McDougal is a *coureur de bois*, a runner of the woods. He's an unlicensed fur trader who tries to steal trade goods from us and cheats the Odawa."

Nicholas's eyes became wide when he finally realized that Meggie and LeClaire were fur traders, like the ones his mother had told him lived along the Grand River and Lake Michigan more than three hundred years ago. Nicholas had heard stories about the *coureur de bois* and how some of them were mean and cheated and stole.

"Why would McDougal want Chris?" Nicholas asked.

"He is a thief and very mean," said LeClaire. "He cannot be trusted. We will go now and find your brother."

Chapter 3
Red Devil and Grey Eyes

Nicholas and LeClaire made their way deep into the cool woods. Old dried leaves, twigs, and brown pine needles, ankle-deep, crackled and snapped beneath their feet. Nicholas followed close behind LeClaire as they walked.

"You make much noise, Little Fawn," LeClaire cautioned . "If McDougal were a bear, he would have eaten you by now."

Nicholas's eyes grew wide at the idea of being eaten by a bear with the name of McDougal. Nicholas understood, however, his new friend was serious.

"Follow close in my steps. I make a quiet path for you to follow." Nicholas walked close behind the giant, stepping in the middle of each spot where LeClaire had stood.

Glad now LeClaire was *un geant* (a giant), Nick could see muscles on his bare arms as he held back branches for Nick to follow under. This giant could put a scare in any Red Devil that would try to take Chris.

The deeper they walked into the forest, the higher the trees loomed around them. They were all great trees, just as Meggie had said. The lowest branches were now high above Nicholas's head, with trunks big enough to stand behind.

"Careful, stay close now, little one. It is easy to see us in this forest." LeClaire traveled carefully from tree to tree, looking around each one before moving to the next.

"Are we close to McDougal's?" Nick whispered.

"*Oui* (yes), we are close. Stay still!"

LeClaire closed his eyes and lifted his head toward the tops of the trees, slowly filling his lungs with deep breaths of air.

"You smell?" LeClaire asked.

"Do I what?" Nicholas questioned.

"Breathe deep. Do you, Little Fawn, smell the odor of furs and grease gone bad? That is the smell of McDougal."

Nick sniffed the air but could only smell the pine trees and warm, moist earth of the forest floor.

Just at that moment, deep thundering laughter like that of a Devil, echoed through the woods. LeClaire pulled Nicholas close behind the trunk of a tree. Once again the laughter burst forth, the terrible sound bouncing around the forest.

"It is Le Diable Rouge, the Red Devil. We are near McDougal's post."

Seeing the look in LeClaire's eyes, Nicholas wondered if this man McDougal might really be a Devil. Nicholas moved closer behind the tree, near LeClaire.

Nick was certain Mom and Dad would be really angry if they knew any of this was going on in the woods near their home. Maybe it was better they didn't. As soon as LeClaire found Chris, they could both go home. No one would have to know about this.

Laughter again filled the air and two voices could plainly be heard. Neither voice, however, was that of Christopher. Maybe Meggie and LeClaire were wrong and Chris wasn't with McDougal.

"Stay close," said LeClaire. "Walk only where I walk, stand only where I stand." LeClaire moved from one tree to the next, waiting each time for Nicholas to follow. Closer and closer they came to the sound of the voices.

Pausing behind a tree, LeClaire motioned to Nicholas. Ahead of them was a clearing with a small log cabin surrounded by big rocks. Making his way to the edge of the forest, LeClaire motioned for Nicholas to stay put.

Nicholas peeked around the side of the tree. The cabin looked old and dirty, with logs of different lengths. Mud was plastered along the sides of the cabin, probably to keep out the cold. An opening cut into the side of the cabin wall served as a window with no glass. Under the window stood a large barrel filled with grimy water. All around the cabin there were large boulders, not big enough to hide behind, but too big to walk over. It appeared the cabin had been built right in the middle of where the rocks stood.

Nicholas pulled back behind the tree and took a deep breath. LeClaire was right, he too could smell McDougal's post. It was an ugly, greasy smell.

Nick peeked out again from behind the tree and could see LeClaire motioning for him. Sneaking carefully across to the next tree,

Nicholas was once again secure beside the gentle giant.

LeClaire now stooped down and crept on all fours to the side of the cabin. He silently edged his way to the water barrel that stood under the window hole.

The voices of the two men were heard again. Nicholas could see the shape of a man walking back and forth inside the cabin. LeClaire crouched flat against the side of the wall as someone moved closer to the window.

Nicholas hugged tight behind the tree and held his breath, hoping neither of them could be seen. After a moment he peeked around the tree, and there standing in the window above LeClaire was a man. It had to be McDougal, because he looked like a Red Devil with wiry red hair and a scruffy red beard. The man stretched his arms and opened his mouth wide, yawning. Nicholas could see the Devil had his two front teeth missing.

LeClaire was crouching as flat against the wall as he could and didn't move a muscle.

McDougal stretched again and left the window. Loud voices again came from inside the cabin. LeClaire edged onto his knees and peeked into the window.

Remaining silent, Nicholas shut his eyes and crossed all his fingers and toes, hoping his giant friend would not be discovered. All of a sudden, a large hand came over Nicholas's mouth and held him tight. Startled, Nick jumped, but it was only LeClaire, who, while Nick's eyes were shut, had returned to the tree.

Releasing his grip, LeClaire motioned for Nicholas to follow him away from the cabin. They stopped a short distance away and LeClaire spoke quietly to Nick. "Do not be afraid by what I tell you. In the cabin there are two Devils. One is my enemy McDougal, the other is Grey Eyes, a bad Métis, who will do anything for the feel of silver in his hand. He comes from across the Great Sea of Michigand, from Ouisconsin."

Nicholas knew by the look in LeClaire's dark eyes that this was not all he had seen.

"There is more. There is a boy, bigger than you. He is tied and has a cloth over his mouth. I think he sleeps."

"You think he sleeps? What do you mean, LeClaire? Is he all right?"

"If he were not," said LeClaire, "they would have no reason to tie him."

Nicholas thought hard for a moment. He could feel tears begin to burn in his eyes.

"Do not be frightened, Nicholas Corey. We will help your brother." LeClaire wiped the tears from Nicholas's eyes with his big, gentle hand.

"You be strong now, like LeClaire. We go to Meggie and decide how best to help your brother. Meggie will want to know of Grey Eyes."

Nicholas followed LeClaire through the woods and back along the path to Meggie's cabin. It seemed to take twice as long as before. Nicholas thought only about Christopher. I wonder what I will do if something bad happens, he asked himself. Maybe he should get the police in Grand Haven. Maybe he should go get his parents.

Soon the smell of Meggie's cabin filled the air, a smell far more pleasing than McDougal's cabin. The two entered to find Meggie standing before the fireplace stirring something in a big black pot that hung over the fire. "Is it true? The boy is with Le Diable Rouge?" asked Meggie.

Nicholas nodded yes.

"*Oui*, Meggie, and the Devil also has a partner, Grey Eyes."

"Grey Eyes. It cannot be!" Meggie steadied herself and sat down on the bench beside the table. "I thought Grey Eyes to be no longer of this world."

Nicholas became frightened by these words. "LeClaire, what does she mean?"

LeClaire looked at Meggie sadly and placed his hand upon her shoulder. "It is Madame's story to tell, Little Fawn."

LeClaire turned to the pot boiling at the fire and dished up two wooden bowls of steaming soup. Placing one before Nicholas, LeClaire pointed to him to eat.

LeClaire lifted his bowl to his mouth and drank the hot soup. "I go outside, Madame. I cut wood for the fire."

Nicholas watched as LeClaire left, closing the door behind him. Soon the chopping sound of an axe cutting wood was heard outside.

"Madame, who is Grey Eyes? Why do he and McDougal want Chris?"

"Drink soup while it's hot. I will tell you my story."

Nicholas drank some of the soup as LeClaire had done. It was hot and it tasted good.

"I hope those men feed Chris. He's probably hungry," Nick thought out loud. "Chris is always hungry."

"They will feed your brother. Do not worry, they will take good care of him. They can sell him for much silver to the British at the fort on the Ile de Michilimackinac. The British use young men at the stone fort to do chores. Now the British will need extra help to pack. Americans will soon come to live at the fort and the British have to leave."

"Sell Chris? They can't do that! It's against the law. I gotta tell my parents so they can call the police. Do you have a phone or a car or some way to get help?"

"There is no help in these woods, Little Fawn. The only help your brother has is us. These men will not stay long in the forest. They know your Christopher is valuable. Someone will be looking for him." Nick felt that Meggie was probably right and he must now trust her and LeClaire to help Chris.

"Let me tell you about these men. McDougal is a *coureur de bois*, who has no right to be in the forest. He has no pass from the brothers of the Three Fires— the Odawa, the Potawatomie, or the Chippewa— to be on their hunting grounds. He has no pass from the Red Coats, the British, who live at the white stone fort on Mackinac. He is bad, this Le Diable Rouge. And Grey Eyes is also bad. He has offended the blood of my family.

"Little Fawn, you say your brother is big and strong. He will bring a good price to the purse of McDougal. The Devil will sell him as a slave. Your brother is safe for the time."

The idea of Chris being sold as a slave didn't make much sense to Nicholas. Chris wouldn't even do the dishes at home unless Mom made him.

"Meggie," Nick asked, "what about this guy Grey Eyes?"

Nick watched Meggie as she walked slowly to the fireplace. There she carefully picked up a shiny silver cross with a black ribbon tied to it that lay on a shelf. Standing silently, she stared at the cross and then gently placed it back in its resting place. Nicholas could now see the tears in Meggie's eyes when she turned around.

"I will tell you about Grey Eyes. He is a Métis like myself, only he is part Winnebago and part French. His people live across the waters of the big lake. He knew my husband's family and tried to kill them for trade goods in Ouisconsin."

My husband, Monsieur La Framboise, my Joseph, was French. His family were traders of fur."

"Wow! My mom told me all sorts of stories about fur traders, but I thought they only lived a long time ago."

"If Grey Eyes tried to hurt your family," Nick continued, "why didn't you have him arrested by the police?"

Meggie narrowed her eyes and looked at Nicholas in a strange way. "What is this police you talk about? Is it a man?"

"It's lots of men. They help people when there's trouble. You don't have police where you come from? They wear uniforms and carry guns and everything," answered Nick.

"Uniforms? What color are these uniforms?" inquired Meggie.

At that moment LeClaire entered the cabin, his arms filled with firewood. Stooping low, he placed the wood in a pile beside the fireplace.

"LeClaire, this boy tells of men who help people when they are troubled by bad men such as Grey Eyes."

LeClaire cocked his head and looked at Nicholas. "Where are these men to be found?"

"LeClaire, beware. They sound like the soldiers of King George. Little Fawn tells me they wear uniforms and carry guns," cautioned Meggie.

"Uniforms of red, Little Fawn?" LeClaire asked as he stood tall over Nicholas. His toothy grin had turned to a frown and his skin glistened with sweat. "You know the soldiers of King George?"

"King who? Police aren't soldiers, and they wear mostly blue uniforms!"

"The blue of the Americans?" Meggie asked firmly.

"Yeah, police are Americans," Nick answered.

"These Americans, are they like you?"

"Only bigger. You gotta be old, maybe in your twenties before you can be a policeman," said Nick.

LeClaire stood and stared at Meggie with a curious look.

"LeClaire, maybe having Americans come live at the Fort will be good. These police will help rid us of men like McDougal."

"They can help get rid of Grey Eyes, too," Nick added. "They'll take him to prison or something. What did he do to offend your blood, anyway?"

"Nicholas, Grey Eyes is a renegade like his brother, White Ox. White Ox is evil and killed my husband many seasons ago," Meggie said sadly.

Nicholas was surprised and now understood why Meggie acted so strangely.

"White Ox and his brother followed my husband from Ouisconsin to Michigand, across the big water. Joseph, my husband, had many posts and many trade goods. White Ox liked the taste of the white man's milk."

Nicholas scrunched his eyes. "What's wrong with liking milk? I like milk."

LeClaire shook his head. "Meggie, the boy thinks you speak of goat's milk."

"*Non, mon ami*, I speak of liquor called rum. It is poison to our people. After they taste rum, it brings out evil spirits, making people do what is not good."

"Yeah, I've heard that happens to a lot of people. We've got laws that are all about people drinking too much milk and stuff like that."

"You understand, White Ox and Grey Eyes, steal and hurt traders for this drink."

Nicholas's mind began to wander thinking about Christopher being in the cabin with this evil Grey Eyes.

"White Ox followed my Joseph to our post," Meggie continued, "near *La Grande Riviére*. I was with my husband at the time."

"*Oui*, and I was also there with other voyageurs," said LeClaire. "Joseph was my best friend. The bad renegades, White Ox and his brother, Grey Eyes, came to our camp demanding white man's milk."

"Joseph was in our tent," Meggie added as she rose from the bench and again reached for the cross that lay on the shelf.

"LeClaire, please finish the story for me. It is too hard."

"*Oui*, Madame. This wild dog, White Ox, and his brother had a plan. Grey Eyes talked to our men about trade while White Ox stole into Monsieur Joseph's tent for rum. Instead of finding rum, he found Joseph. White Ox attacked Joseph."

"My husband was a good man," Meggie added. "He never carried liquor. White Ox wanted to even the score with Joseph for the trouble in Ouisconsin. He pulled his knife and killed my Joseph. I came to the tent and found my husband lying on the ground, holding his cross."

Meggie held the cross high into the air by its ribbon. "This is the cross of my husband. It reminds me always to keep a strong heart." As she looked at the cross, tears ran down her face.

"In the trouble, Grey Eyes ran from camp," LeClaire continued. "Before his escape, however, he was cut by the knife of one of the voyageurs. He carries the scar across his face that tells everyone of his evil deed. White Ox was not so fortunate. He was found lying in the forest without his spirit."

"LeClaire, we've got to hurry and get Chris before something bad happens." Nicholas jumped to his feet.

"We make a plan now, Little Fawn. Your brother will be fine."

Meggie began gathering things from around the little cabin and putting them in order. "I will make ready to leave for the Ile De Michili-mackinac. We will need the help from the soldiers at the stone fort, after your brother is safe in our canoe. The Red Coats may not be our friends, but they have rules like your police. They say every trader must have permission to trade in this territory. They also know of Grey Eyes and his evil deeds. My Joseph was a friend to the people of Mackinac. They will help us."

Meggie reached into a large basket and pulled out pieces of soft brown leather and laid them on the table before Nicholas. "This is for you and your brother. They are moccasins. They will help you both run swiftly and silently through the forest."

Nicholas picked up the soft leather slippers, remembering Christopher was barefoot and how much noise his own shoes made in the woods.

"Aki, Mother Earth, will keep you safe as long as you can feel her beneath your feet," said Meggie.

"It is good you rest now," LeClaire urged, and he pulled a big shaggy black fur from out of a box. "Sleep before the fire, on my bear robe. I will wake you when it is time to leave."

Nicholas lay down and wrapped the soft robe around him. As he started to relax, he remembered his magic turtle warrior rock. Pulling it from his pocket, he could see its legs stretched out in all four directions with a little bump of stone that resembled a turtle's head looking up to the sky.

I hope this warrior can help Chris, Nick thought to himself. Holding the stone tightly in his hand, he watched the flames in the fireplace and quietly drifted off to sleep.

Chapter 4
The Rescue

The sun cast weird shadows in the woods when Nicholas and LeClaire began their journey back to McDougal's post. Nick was glad he had rested. He hoped Christopher would also be rested so he would be ready when the time came to make his escape.

This time the trail to McDougal's post seemed shorter. Nick followed close behind LeClaire, walking silently through the woods in his new moccasins. Every so often, LeClaire stopped and lifted his head toward the treetops, trying to smell his way to the Red Devil's post.

Soon McDougal's cabin came in view. Listening carefully, both Nicholas and LeClaire could hear the voices from inside the cabin. This time, however, they could also hear Christopher's voice. "I don't know what you guys want. I'm no spy. And if you don't let me go, the police will be here soon and you'll be sorry."

"Be quiet you American dog!" snapped the gravelly voice of McDougal. "Ye say ye ain't no spy. Well, then let's see if you can cook." The voices of the two men raised into laughter.

Nicholas looked at LeClaire, wondering how they were going to get Christopher free from these crazy men. Just then LeClaire pulled Nicholas close to the trunk of the tree. A form appeared in the window hole. It was the renegade, Grey Eyes.

"Cooking is a good job for this slave," said Grey Eyes. "Slave, go get water from this barrel to cook our soup." Grey Eyes motioned with his hand out the window toward the barrel that stood just below the window hole.

LeClaire looked down at Nicholas. Nicholas knew he had to be very quiet. How were they going to let Christopher know they were there to rescue him? Chris must be really scared, thought Nick. He needs to know we are here.

Nick paused a moment and then gently worked his way from beside LeClaire along the tree. Before LeClaire could stop him, Nicholas shot from behind the tree, dashing to the side of the cabin. There he squatted low, edging his way to the window, hugging close to the water barrel. He had to let Christopher know he was there!

LeClaire watched as Nicholas reached into his pocket, carefully pulling something out and putting it beside the barrel. On all fours, Nicholas scurried back to LeClaire and the safety of the trees.

"What have you done, you imp?" growled LeClaire in a low voice. "What if you had been seen? What if you were caught? Then there would be two of you to rescue." LeClaire stared deep into Nicholas's eyes with a ferocious look. "What was it you left beside the barrel?"

"LeClaire, it's OK. It's a special rock. Chris knows it's mine. He's got to get water from that barrel, right? He'll see the rock and know I'm here."

LeClaire and Nicholas turned their attention back to the cabin. They could see Grey Eyes pull Christopher to his feet, and then take his long hunting knife and cut the ties that held Chris's hands. Christopher walked slowly, as if he had been tied into knots for a long time. In his hands he carried a large wooden bucket.

Grey Eyes again stood at the window, watching Chris. "Do not think to escape, American. The bears will eat you!"

McDougal chimed in, "If a bear eats that boy, Grey Eyes, I'll take twenty-five pounds of silver from your hide."

Christopher slowly looked around as he lowered the bucket into the water.

Nick crossed his fingers and chanted to himself. "Look down, Chris, look down. You've got to see the rock."

Chris took his time filling the bucket, glancing toward the woods, looking for a way of escape.

LeClaire quietly whispered, "Your brother, he does not see the rock."

Chris lifted the bucket, heavy with water from the barrel. Stepping backward, he was careful not to spill it. Just then, Chris's bare foot stepped back, right on top of the turtle warrior.

All right, that's my brother, Nick thought. He always steps on my rocks!

Stumbling, Chris caught his balance and quickly sat down, rubbing his foot.

"See the rock, see the rock," Nick whispered. LeClaire glared down at Nicholas to be quiet.

It was then Christopher spied the turtle warrior. Picking it up, he realized immediately what it was and quickly slipped it into his pants' pocket. Looking in all directions, he searched the woods for Nicholas.

"What is it you have?" snapped Grey Eyes, who now stood above Chris. Chris quickly stood, picking up the bucket.

"You put something in your clothes, American, what was it?" Grey Eyes growled as he spoke to Chris.

"It's nothing, really." Christopher started to walk around Grey Eyes, holding the heavy bucket tight to his body.

"If it's nothing, then why do you hide it in your clothes?" Grey Eyes reached for Christopher.

This was the first time Nicholas had had a chance to see the renegade up close. He was taller than Chris, but not as tall as LeClaire, and his long black hair hung loose across his shoulders.

"Show me what you have, American dog!" Grey Eyes shook Chris by the arm.

LeClaire reached for Nicholas and placed his hand tightly over his mouth. Nick could not move or make a sound. He could not help Chris now, no matter what happened.

"Let go of me, you jerk," shouted Chris, "I said it was nothing."

Christopher pulled away from Grey Eyes. Grey Eyes grabbed him again, this time splashing the whole pail of water on both of them.

Dripping wet, Grey Eyes was filled with anger. He reached behind his back and pulled his long hunting knife from his belt. Chris froze to the spot, not daring to move an inch. They both faced each other, water dripping from their clothes.

Nick tried to squirm free of LeClaire. He had to help his brother. LeClaire held tight, not letting Nick move or make a sound. Finally Nick gave up.

"Grey Eyes," came a booming, gravelly voice from the door of the cabin. "Ye got twenty-five pounds of silver to give me? 'Cause if ye ain't, put that knife back in yer belt." McDougal stood with his wiry red hair sticking out in all directions and in his hands he held a long gun.

Grey Eyes, startled by McDougal, turned quickly and faced the Red Devil with the knife in his hand. Angered by McDougal, Grey Eyes glared like a wild animal.

McDougal lifted his gun. "Ye don't want me to use this, now do ye, partner?" he asked with a gleam in his eyes. Grey Eyes threw his head back giving out a wild howl like that of a wolf.

McDougal lowered the rifle, and laughed. "What's this about?"

"The boy hides something in his clothes." Grey Eyes turned, jabbing his knife toward Christopher, then placed it in his belt pocket.

For the first time Chris was glad McDougal was there. He was still standing in his frozen state, not sure what to do next. "Boy, what is it ye have that so frightened the great Grey Eyes?" McDougal asked mocking Grey Eyes.

"It's nothing, really," said Chris. "It's just a rock. A little rock. Here, look." Chris dropped the empty bucket and reached into his wet pocket, pulling out the turtle warrior.

McDougal ripped the rock from Chris's grasp and carefully examined it.

"I like rocks," said Chris. Look, you can see it looks like a turtle. See, the legs and the head." Chris was glad he remembered why Nick wanted to keep the rock.

McDougal laughed loudly, opening his mouth so wide that the gap between his teeth could be seen. "The lad's right, ol' Grey, it's a turtle.

Your people have special meaning for the turtle don't they, Grey Eyes? Take a look."

Grey Eyes pulled back with anger and turned from McDougal. "You are a fool, McDougal. The boy here has a rock to break our skulls when we are not looking."

"This is no weapon now, is it lad?" McDougal looked deep into Chris's eyes for the truth. "This is no weapon against the likes of a man such as me and my friend here, now is it?

"No sir, I just like rocks, that's all." Chris shrugged his shoulders and hung his head low.

For a second Nicholas thought he could see tears forming in his brother's eyes. LeClaire, who was still holding Nicholas tightly, released his grip.

"Grey Eyes," McDougal continued. "The boy likes rocks. It can't be you're so jumpy because ye got a bath a few months early, can it?"

Grey Eyes turned and lunged toward Christopher, growling in his face like an animal.

"That ye'll not be doin'!" yelled McDougal and pushed Grey Eyes back. "This boy is worth his health in silver to the Brits, and I'll not be havin' ye damage him before I collect for my trouble. Do ye hear, me ye renegade dog, do ye?"

Grey Eyes stood back, throwing his loose hair over his shoulder, and laughed at Christopher. It was then Nicholas could see the long jagged scar that marked Grey Eyes' face, put there by Joseph's voyageur many years ago.

"Hear me, Grey Eyes, I want ye ta be nice to the lad. Give the boy back his little rock." McDougal grinned, the gaping hole from his missing teeth, showing wide.

Grey Eyes glared at McDougal, grabbing the rock from him. He pushed it into Chris's face. Christopher slowly reached out and took the rock, placing it back in his pocket.

"Ye be careful, lad, he ain't take a likin' to ye like I have," said McDougal, as he pulled his knife from his belt and cut two long leather pieces of fringe from the side of his buckskin jacket. "Ye know, lad, ye best stay outside for a while, up by this here little tree. That way ol' Grey can settle himself a little." McDougal pulled Christopher between two large boulders to a small pine tree that grew close to the edge of the forest.

"Put yer hands behind ye so I can tie 'em."

Christopher quickly obeyed as the Red Devil tied the fringe pieces tightly together making a leather rope to tie Chris to the sapling.

"Now ye be still, lad, so ol' Grey will forget about ye. I know'd the skeeters will be bad, but it might be just the thing to make ol' Grey feel better about the bath ye gave him."

Nick watched silently as McDougal left Christopher tied to the tree. Looking up to LeClaire, he knew this was going to be the chance they needed to free Chris.

From the cabin, Grey Eyes and McDougal could be heard arguing. Soon the argument came to an end and the smell of rancid grease frying filled the air.

Nick watched as Christopher slipped down the small tree and leaned forward struggling to loosen his hands.

"When your brother fights no more, that will be the time for me to go to him," LeClaire whispered to Nick.

LeClaire placed his hands on Nicholas's shoulders and looked deeply into his eyes. "Little Fawn," he whispered, "you must trust me, I am your friend."

Nicholas nodded his head "Yes."

"Then, will you do what I tell you?" Nicholas thought for a moment and wondered what it was LeClaire was about to ask.

"I want you to go away from this cabin. Be careful not to stumble over the rocks or in the bushes. Do not make noise. Go to the woods the way we came. Hide there, wait for your brother to come to you."

"But I can help, LeClaire," Nicholas whispered as softly as he could.

"You can help by being in the forest waiting to greet your brother. He does not know me, he might fight with me. Do you remember how you tried to fight when we met?"

Nicholas, ashamed of how he had acted, nodded his head and looked up at LeClaire. "Help Chris, OK?"

"Help Chris, OK!" repeated LeClaire. "Now go, and do not look back. Hide until you see us approach."

Nicholas could see that Christopher had now stopped struggling with his bindings. The time was near. He would have to trust LeClaire, the gentle giant, his friend.

LeClaire gave Nicholas a grin and pointed in the direction of the woods. "Be careful, Nicholas Corey."

The forest had started to grow dark since they had arrived at the cabin. Nicholas walked carefully, watching for rocks and bushes, walking as silently as he could, as LeClaire had taught him. Nicholas walked away from the cabin until he could no longer smell the stink of McDougal's post.

The buzz of mosquitoes swirled around his head and, with evening the forest was full of hoots and howls, sounds coming from all sorts of animals. Feeling sad and all alone, Nicholas thought about home. He knew his parents would be home now. They were probably calling all of his friends, trying to find where he and Chris were playing. Nick wished with all his might that he and Chris were home safe, washing up for supper.

It seemed like forever Nick sat in the woods, swatting giant mosquitoes and fighting back tears.

Suddenly Nick could hear something coming through the underbrush. It must be Chris with

LeClaire. Then the noise stopped. Nick ducked close beside the tree. Maybe it's a bear, or worse yet, Grey Eyes, he thought to himself.

Peeking out from around the tree, Nicholas could see a shadowy figure coming toward him. Nicholas stood quietly, getting ready to run. At that moment, Chris's voice broke the silence. "Nick, are you there?" Chris whispered loudly.

Nicholas jumped from behind his tree, giving Chris a fright. The two boys hugged, glad to be together again. "Nick, you're not going to believe what happened!" Chris started talking excitedly. "I was running down the path to the tree and—"

Just then LeClaire silently appeared out of the forest and reached forth with his long arm, putting his hand to Chris's mouth. "You must be silent, you are not away from danger yet. Follow the trail back to Madame's post. I will meet you along the trail. I have to finish my work." LeClaire again disappeared in the direction of McDougal's post.

"LeClaire," Nick called quietly, "Thank you." Nicholas grabbed Chris's hand, leading him away from danger.

"Nick, slow up, I don't have shoes on," whispered Chris.

Nick had forgotten in all the excitement that Christopher was still barefoot. Reaching deep into his shirt, he pulled out the second pair of moccasins that Meggie had given him for Chris.

"Here, put these on, they'll help." Chris pulled the leather slippers onto his feet and followed Nicholas through the woods.

"Nick, who was that guy? He came out of nowhere, put his hand over my mouth, and cut my ties. I bet those two jerks don't even know I'm gone yet.

"Boy am I glad you got that turtle rock. I recognized it right off. I knew you had to be around some place. We've got to get home, Mom and Dad are gonna be worried. When they find out what happened, we'll be grounded forever."

"Chris," Nick urged, "be quiet. I'll explain everything when we get to Meggie's."

"Meggie's?" said Chris loudly. Just then a big hand again came down around Christopher's mouth, holding him tight.

"Do you want to be found out? Do you want to be sold as a servant for the rest of your life?" LeClaire had caught up with the boys again.

"I tried to tell him," Nick whispered to LeClaire.

"You be silent too, Little Fawn, follow close behind." Nick and Chris followed silently behind LeClaire as they made their way back to Meggie's cabin.

Chapter 5
The Reunion

As they approached, Nicholas was glad to see the warm, orange glow of the fireplace from the window of Meggie's cabin. Sniffing the air, he could smell soup cooking. "Come on, Chris, you gotta meet Meggie."

LeClaire opened the door of the cabin wide, and Meggie quickly turned from her work at the fireplace.

"You are back, and you have brought the explorer Christopher with you. You see, Little Fawn, I told you LeClaire would help." Meggie smiled and ruffled Nicholas's hair with her hand.

"Chris, I would like you to meet my two new friends—Madame La Framboise (you can call her Meggie), and LeClaire, the giant." Nick smiled. He was glad he and Chris were now safe in Meggie's cabin.

Chris looked at Meggie and LeClaire and then at Nicholas.

"Chris, what's the matter with you?" asked Nicholas. "Can't you say hello? After all, they did help rescue you."

Meggie smiled at Christopher. "Perhaps your brother would like something to eat before we leave."

"It's nice to meet you all." said Chris. "Nick, you told these people I'm an explorer?"

LeClaire laughed loudly. "The boy has the same look the Little Fawn had when we first met."

"Little Fawn! They call you Little Fawn?" Chris laughed. "That's a good one. I like that, Little Fawn."

"Knock it off, Chris, it's not funny." Nick shook his head and gave his brother a cross look.

"It's really nice to meet you all, and thanks for helping me out back there. You know, you're pretty strong looking, LeClaire. Have you ever played any pro football?"

LeClaire smiled and shrugged his shoulders.

"Chris," said Nick, "something really strange has happened to us this afternoon."

"You're telling me! When Mom and Dad find out about all this, we're gonna be in big trouble.

"Chris, you don't understand. These people are fur traders."

"Wow, that's nice, I bet they have some nice coats for the winter. But Nick, we've got to go!"

Meggie and LeClaire stared at the boys, trying to understand all the things that were said.

"Well, what do you think, Little Fawn? What are we gonna tell Mom and Dad about this? I'd sure like to see those guys, especially that dude with the long black hair, get arrested by the police. Wouldn't you? That Grey Eyes guy was really nuts."

Meggie shook her head in amazement and went to the fireplace to dish up bowls of soup.

"Chris, don't you understand? Something really strange is going on here," Nick insisted.

"Strange! Things can't get much stranger, Nick."

"Chris, I can't explain this, but it was like when I found the turtle warrior rock and knew it was special."

"Yeah, well, it is special. If it wasn't for that rock, I wouldn't be here with you now," said Chris. "That reminds me, here's your little buddy." Chris dug deep into his pocket and pulled out the turtle rock, handing it to Nick.

"Chris," Nick insisted, "don't you think it's weird that we are in a cabin in the middle of the woods? The middle of our woods by our house? A

cabin we've never seen before? And Meggie—
she's a Métis. She's part French and part Indian.
And LeClaire is from Port Royal and used to be a
slave."

"We've got French in us, too. Mom told me
so," Chris added.

"What about McDougal wanting to sell you
at Mackinac Island? You've got to admit, Chris,
something weird is happening. When was the last
time you heard of fur traders along Lake
Michigan?"

Chris started to laugh, "About three hundred
years ago."

"That's what I mean. I think we've gone back
in time."

Chris could tell by the look on Nick's face that
he was serious, but it was all too much for Chris
to believe.

"Come on Nick, how could anyone travel back
in time? That stuff happens in movies and books,
not real life. You know, I think we should
probably just go home. Mom and Dad will be
upset enough that we are late." Chris put his arm
around Nick, trying to make him feel better.

Nicholas knew it wasn't going to be quite so easy. "Chris, the police here are British soldiers. And do you see a light switch, a telephone, or even a bathroom?"

"Knock it off, Nick! You're not funny any more."

"You know, Meggie thought we were real explorers. LeClaire thought I was an American spy. McDougal and Grey Eyes are illegal fur traders and wanted to sell you at Mackinac."

Chris looked around the little cabin and for the first time realized there wasn't a phone, television, electric lights, or a bathroom.

LeClaire and Meggie, who sat at the table talking quietly between themselves in French, sipped their soup from wooden bowls.

"Boys," Meggie said, "you must eat before it is time to leave. The woods are getting dark, but at the beach the sun has not yet set. McDougal will be onto us soon and our trip to the Ile de Michilimackinac is a long journey."

"Come on, Chris, we might as well eat. There isn't anything else we can do." Nick and Chris sat down at the table and Meggie filled their bowls with soup.

"LeClaire," Nick asked. "Why did you leave us after you helped Chris escape? You said you had work to finish."

LeClaire's black eyes flashed, and a grin came to his face. Wiping his mouth on the back of his hand, LeClaire reached behind his back and pulled out a long knife from his belt.

"You see, Grey Eyes is not the only renegade to have a knife in these woods," LeClaire laughed. "I crept back to McDcugal's post and slashed the bottom of his canoe. I did this so the Red Devil could not follow us when we left for the Ile de Michilimackinac."

"May I see your knife, LeClaire?" Chris asked.

LeClaire hesitated and looked deep into Christopher's eyes. "You like my knife? You must handle it carefully, it is very sharp." LeClaire presented Christopher the handle of the knife. The knife was heavy, with a long, blue steel blade.

"Wow, this is great. A real trader's hunting knife." Chris examined the knife and then handed it back to LeClaire.

"LeClaire," Chris said, "you guys don't have police around here? I know Grand Haven has a police station."

"*Oui*, your brother has spoken of these men in uniform and the place called Grand Haven. This Grand Haven you speak of we do not know. He also tells us these police are Americans, and the Americans are not due to come to the island until the end of the Strawberry moon (June). That is a while off."

Chris had a surprised look on his face.

"I told you, Chris," jeered Nick.

"Nick, I think you and I should go home now. Mom and Dad are going to be real worried if we don't show up soon."

Meggie rose from the table and picked up the wooden soup bowls and placed them in a bucket of water by the fire.

"I believe it would be wise for you to be with your parents," said Meggie, "but LeClaire and I do not know how to find your parents. We do not know of your American police and we have never heard of this place called Grand Haven.

"LeClaire and I have worked in this area ever since my husband was killed by White Ox. The only settlement that is near is that called Gabagouache, an Odawa Indian settlement. The Odawas are not there at this time. They too have gone to the Ile to rendezvous.

"I believe, my young friends, you are lost. And I know that my enemy Grey Eyes and the Red Devil will soon be looking for you. You must understand the Ile de Michilimackinac will be the only safe place for you. The soldiers there, like your police, will help us."

"McDougal will soon know you are missing," said LeClaire. "He will look for you. He will use his nose to find his way to Madame's cabin. We must leave soon."

Nick looked at Chris to see if he understood. "He'll be able to smell Meggie's soup in the air, the way we could smell the Red Devil's stinky supper." Chris shook his head, remembering the ugly smells inside McDougal's cabin.

LeClaire stood up from the table and stretched, reaching so high he touched the wooden beams that lined the ceiling. He rubbed his stomach and belched loudly.

The boys laughed and Meggie smiled. "LeClaire, you sound as if your belly would explode. You must be quiet, or your stomach sounds will lead the Red Devil to our cabin."

Meggie and the boys laughed. LeClaire smiled and patted his stomach again.

"Meggie," said LeClaire, "I will go secure the canoe. Make ready to leave. You and the boys prepare. Come to the canoe soon." LeClaire closed the door tightly behind him and Meggie doused the fire with water.

"Nick, I don't know about all this," said Chris in a worried voice.

"I don't think we have a choice," said Nick. "We are gonna have to trust Meggie and LeClaire. And anyway we are going to have to get down to the lake to get into the canoe. If we see the lights from Grand Haven, we can make a run for it, OK?"

Chris felt better knowing that if they hadn't traveled back in time, they would have a chance to run for home. Meggie gave the boys two small bundles wrapped in white cloth.

"This is food for our trip, dried meat and berries. It is good." Meggie again stirred the smoldering fire as puffs of smoke and sparks flew into the air and up the chimney. "All is ready. We go."

"I promise," said Meggie, "I will get you help so that we can find your parents. We are safe together." Chris and Nick felt Meggie meant her promise and for the first time Christopher thought they might be doing the right thing.

Meggie slung a bundle across her shoulders, and the three of them left the cabin, making their way through the dark forest. It wasn't long before they came to an immense clearing. There the shadows of the woods gave way to a sky filled with an orange and red sunset. They stood at the edge of a dune, looking down the great hill of sand. At the bottom the sand flattened out, forming a field of beach grass as far as the eye could see. And across the middle of the field of grass, flowed a wide river.

"Nick, I have never seen this place before, have you?" For a moment the boys stared out from their perch atop the dune. Searching in all directions, they looked for the lights of the city of Grand Haven.

"Little Fawn, you must hurry this way," called Meggie. She signaled for the boys to follow her over a knoll leading down toward the river.

Following Meggie, they watched for any familiar sign. All they could see, however, was tall beach grass blowing in the gentle breeze.

As they walked along the crest of the dune, the boys could see the river as it cut in and out around small islands of grass and sand, spreading wide to join the mouth of the great Lake Michigan.

"Gabagouache!" whispered Nick.

Meggie stopped and turned. "*Oui,* that is Gabagouache. You see, no one here. They all go to rendezvous. *Le rivière est La Grand Rivière.*

"Grand River, Nick. This is the Grand River," said Chris. "But where are all the houses and restaurants? Where's our house?"

Chris stood for a long time looking out over the sand. A sick feeling came to the pit of his stomach, and for the first time he believed he really had gone back in time.

"We must hurry," said Meggie. "LeClaire waits for us in the canoe." Meggie turned and carefully started down the great hill of sand toward the river. Nick followed, picking his feet up high and throwing sand in all directions. Chris soon joined in and began running down the hill, gaining speed with each step.

Forgetting their troubles for a moment, Chris and Nick tripped each other and rolled down the hill to the beach grass below. They stood laughing and pushing, shaking sand out of their hair and clothes and dusting off the bundles Meggie had given them. Nick rubbed the sand off his face and spit it from his mouth.

"Nick, you gotta learn to shut your mouth. You always have it open. How does the sand taste?"

Nick picked up a handful of sand and started to throw it at Chris. Just then the boys saw Meggie coming toward them, retracing her steps back up from the river. We're in trouble now, Chris thought. Meggie passed by without saying a word and started back up the dune. "Boys," she called back, "follow the path to the canoe."

Chris and Nick dusted the sand from their clothes and shook out their hair. They followed the path that lead through the grass to a flat sandy area. LeClaire was standing in the river with water up to his knees, holding the canoe steady.

"Where is Meggie going?" asked Nicholas.

"Madame has forgotten her husband's cross. She will return soon."

"Her cross? That cross must be really special for her to climb all the way back up that dune to get it," Chris commented.

"It really is, Chris, it means a lot to her." Nicholas dusted the sides of his jeans and unrolled his cuffs, which were full of sand. At the same time he patted his pocket to make sure the turtle warrior was still there.

LeClaire steadied the canoe and the two boys carefully stepped in. "Step in the middle, on the boards," said LeClaire, "then kneel on the floor."

"This is the biggest canoe I've ever seen. What kind is it, LeClaire?" asked Nick.

"This a big *canot* (canoe), *non*, this is *petit* (small) *canot*. A *nord* (north) *canot*, is only twenty-six feet long. Monsieur Red Devil, he has big *canot*, a Montreal, it is thirty-five feet long. I had a lot of work to slash that one with my knife." The three laughed at the joke LeClaire had played on McDougal.

"How big is Grey Eye's canoe?" asked Chris.

"Grey Eyes has no *canot*!" insisted LeClaire.

"Yes, he does. I saw him carrying one up by the cabin right after McDougal grabbed me in the woods. It was smaller than this one, though. He carried it by himself on his shoulders."

LeClaire was upset. "*Sacré* ! This is not good news. We must leave." Just then the boys spotted Meggie making her way down the dune. She was running very fast and waving her arms.

LeClaire pushed the canoe off and climbed into the back. Reaching out with a long red paddle, he pushed the canoe farther away from the shore, directing it into the flow of the river toward Lake Michigan.

"LeClaire, we have to wait for Meggie," Chris demanded.

LeClaire paid no attention and handed the boys paddles. "Start paddling so we catch the current," snapped LeClaire.

Startled by LeClaire's command, Chris and Nick picked up the red tipped paddles and dipped them into the water.

"Get high on your knees and paddle like good voyageurs," called LeClaire.

The boys turned to watch Meggie run down the dune and disappear into the tall beach grass.

"What about Meggie?" asked Nick.

"Paddle, paddle," urged LeClaire.

The canoe rounded a bend in the river and then made its way toward the mouth of the river, where it flows into Lake Michigan. The boys searched the shore, looking for any signs of Meggie in the tall grass along the water's edge. And there, standing on a fallen tree that hung out over the water, stood Meggie.

"Meggie! Look, Chris. There's Meggie!" Nick waved his paddle high into the air.

LeClaire stuck his long paddle out deeply across the surface of the water, directing the canoe toward Meggie.

Stepping gently into the canoe, Meggie exclaimed, "I thought you never come to get me!" The boys could see the twinkle in her eyes and knew this must be a game that the two of them often played.

Meggie knelt on the floor of the canoe, picked up a red tipped paddle, and dipped it into the water. Chris and Nick were glad Meggie was again with them. They were just beginning to realize how scary an adventure they were on.

"LeClaire, we must hurry," said Meggie. "McDougal and Grey Eyes were at the cabin. They were looking for the boy. When I approached, they were fighting over the jug of cider. They must have thought it was a jug of white man's milk."

Nick turned to Chris and whispered, "That's what they call rum."

"I could not get to the cabin to get my Joseph's cross," Meggie said sadly as she stared ahead and dipped her paddle into the water.

"The pendant will be safe, Madame. It is us we must worry about. The boy Christopher tells that Grey Eyes has a canoe hidden at the post. Those two Devils will soon know where to find us."

Meggie nodded her head as she pulled herself close to the side of the canoe and dipped her paddle deep into the water. There ahead of them the boys could see the water of the Grand River mixing with the deeper water of the great Lake Michigan. Where the two waters met, great waves formed white peaks and slapped against one another.

"We must all paddle together, work together so we can cut faster into the waves," called LeClaire.

The birchbark canoe cut into the peaked waves, which threw it into the air, and then dropped it down again with a huge splash. LeClaire reached out his paddle, changing the canoe's direction so that it could ride the waves away from land and the mouth of the Grand River.

Chris and Nick fought their fear and held tightly to their paddles. Following the rhythm Meggie set for them, they all paddled together. As soon as they cleared the rough waters, Chris and Nick looked back along the sandy shore where the wild grasses danced in the wind. Back there, somewhere, Grey Eyes and the Red Devil were looking for Chris. And back there, sometime in the future, would be a city called Grand Haven.

Chapter 6

The Chase

The sun was bright pink and orange as it hung in the sky, preparing to sink below the horizon of Lake Michigan. It's beautiful, thought Nick, as the birchbark canoe cut through the choppy waters near the coastline. Tall sand dunes, pink from the sun's reflection, lined the lakeshore. Forest trees peeked out along the tops of the hills of sand. As far as the eye could see, beach grass grew tall and waved back and forth in the breeze. Nowhere was there a sign of modern life, not a town or a city. No city lights reflected into the sky. No beeps of car horns or buzzing of airplanes could be heard.

The boys, tired of paddling, could feel the tightness of the muscles in their arms and back. Their hands were red and stinging, warning them blisters would soon appear.

"Can't we rest?" asked Nick. "My hands and arms hurt."

"Yeah, mine too," said Chris.

Meggie turned and called to LeClaire. "We take a pipe."

LeClaire steered the canoe into deeper water where the waves were calmer and not so high. There he steadied the canoe with his long paddle. Meggie pulled her paddle from the water and motioned the boys to do the same.

"What's a pipe, Meggie?" asked Nick.

"A pipe is a time of rest for a voyageur or canoe man. Once every hour while traveling the waterway, the canoe men stop for a pipe. The men rest their muscles for the time it takes a pipe to burn."

"Little Fawn, do your hands hurt from the paddle?" asked LeClaire.

"Yeah," said Nick.

"Mine too," added Chris. "I think I'm getting a blister."

LeClaire handed the boys a small, round tin. "Rub this into your hands. It will help."

Chris took the tin and pulled off the lid. "Yuck, this smells bad! What is it?"

Meggie laughed as she watched the faces of the two boys. "I think they do not like your bear grease, *mon ami*."

"Bear grease, yuck!" said Nick.

"It smells not so good, but it will help your hands to make callus, not blisters. It is an old trick," said LeClaire.

The boys dug their fingers into the thick, gooey gel and rubbed it into their hands. It did make their hands feel better, if they could just get used to the smell. Chris returned the tin to LeClaire.

"How many miles can a canoe man or voyageur paddle in a day?" Nick asked Meggie.

LeClaire cleared his throat and splashed water from the tip of his red paddle on the boys. "Why, Little Fawn, do you not ask me? I am the greatest of all voyageurs. I have paddled from far away in the *pays du haut* (the north country) to Quebec, and on all the great waters of the Territory. I am the best of the best. I am strong and big, not like the puny little Frenchmen that paddle their canoes."

"Where did you come from LeClaire? Aren't you French?" Nick asked.

"I was born in Port Royal, a French province of New France (Canada). My mother was a black servant who came to this land with a family from Paris, France. My papa was an African prince brought to this land by Dutch slavers. I am a freeman because my brave papa gave his life to save his master in a fight with the British. I am French by my mama, but my spirit is African, like a warrior. That is why I paddle twenty leagues in the time it takes the sun to travel across the sky."

"Wow, what a story! My mom said we have lots of different kinds of blood in us too, but I don't think we have any African," said Nick.

"That's probably why you're so puny," Chris laughed. "LeClaire, a league is about three miles, isn't it?" asked Chris. "You can paddle sixty miles in one day? That's incredible!"

"LeClaire is a giant, and he is strong," said Meggie. "He is a good partner for me. He is so strong, I often need only LeClaire to help me in my work. He was my husband's best friend."

"LeClaire, it is time that you put your strength to work. We must move on. It will be dark soon. We will make the *Mastigon* and make camp there."

"*Oui*, Madame," said LeClaire, "is it not time for an offering?" LeClaire passed a leather pouch forward to Christopher and pointed to Meggie. "Give this to Madame. She will make an offering for a safe passage."

Christopher gave the leather pouch to Meggie who stood up carefully in the front of the canoe and opened the bag. From it she pulled out something that looked like a piece of dry, brown rope.

Nick turned to LeClaire, "What's that?"

"It is a twist of tobacco. Madame will scatter it to the wind in the four sacred directions and ask for a safe trip upon the waters for our journey. This is something special Madame learned from her Indian mama."

Meggie stood silently and lifted her arms to the sky and scattered broken pieces of the tobacco twist into the air. She did that four times, moving carefully in the canoe to face north, south, east, and west. Each time she stood with her eyes closed and sang an Indian song as she threw tobacco onto the water. When she finished, Meggie returned the pouch to LeClaire.

She smiled at the boys and whispered to them, "You see, tobacco can be used for many things."

Meggie picked up her paddle and positioned herself along the side of the canoe, signaling for the boys to do the same. The waters of the great lake seemed calmer now, and it was easier to paddle. Maybe it was the bear grease, thought Nick, or maybe the tobacco.

Deep below in the clear blue-green water, Chris could see shadows of large fish passing under the canoe. Some of them were as big as Nick. The water was clear and cold.

Licking his lips, Chris thought, it would be nice to have a cool drink of water. Pulling his paddle into the canoe, he dipped his hand into the waves, and tried to catch a handful of water. The cold waves splashed up his arm and slapped him in the face with none reaching his mouth.

Just then, he felt a thump across his shoulders. It was LeClaire. There, dangling from the end of his long paddle, was the red canteen.

"My canteen! Where'd you find it?"

"LeClaire found it in the woods," said Nick, "right before he found me."

"Thanks, LeClaire. I thought I had lost this." Unscrewing the lid, Chris took a long drink. When he finished, he passed it to Nick, who also drank.

The water tasted like home and the boys couldn't help but wonder what their parents were doing right then. It sure would be nice, Chris thought, to be standing in the kitchen at home getting a drink of water.

The waves splashed up into the canoe as LeClaire changed direction with his long paddle, cutting across at an angle closer to the shoreline.

"Why don't you have a motor for this canoe? It's big enough for a motor, isn't it?" asked Nick.

"Nick," said Chris, "I don't think fur traders used motors. I don't even think they are invented yet."

"What is this motor?" questioned LeClaire.

"Well, it's this thing that hooks to the back of your boat. It has a propeller, like a fan that spins around. It pushes the boat through the water. It goes real fast and you don't have to paddle."

"Do Americans have these motors?" asked Meggie.

"Yeah," said Chris, "lots of motors are made in America." Our dad has a motorboat, and he takes us for rides all the time. Last summer I even got to steer the boat when we went out fishing." Chris smiled, remembering how much fun he had had fishing with his dad. But they had never caught any fish as big as the ones he had seen in the lake today.

"Americans must be smart to put motors on canoes. I think I will be happy when the Americans come to the Ile de Michilimackinac."

Meggie turned smiling at Chris. As she looked beyond the canoe, however, her expression quickly changed to fear.

"What is it?" questioned LeClaire as he steadied the canoe. Chris and Nick turned, and there in the distance, on the shore, something shiny flashed and then was gone.

Once again they saw the flash. Meggie, standing carefully in the canoe, gazed at the shore. "It is McDougal!" she cried. "Something hangs from his neck."

Staring hard, Meggie recognized the familiar design. "It is the cross of my Joseph that catches the sunset!"

Meggie quickly turned and kneeled in the canoe, taking up her paddle. The others joined her, splashing the water with their red paddles and pushing the canoe forward as fast as they could.

"Madame," LeClaire called, "Joseph's cross has saved us from these renegades. It is a sign we will be safe! I do not think they could see us. They were looking along the shore."

"*Oui*," called Meggie. "We must hurry to the cove of Mastigon."

Chapter 7

The Cove

The canoe cut quickly through the water as the paddles pulled it forward.

"Mastigon is not far, Madame," called LeClaire. "We have not long to paddle."

The wind blew from behind the canoe, helping them move faster. I hope LeClaire is right, thought Chris, as he wondered if McDougal and Grey Eyes had seen them on the water. Perhaps McDougal was searching the shoreline, thinking he and Nick would be too afraid to canoe the big waters.

Meggie pulled her paddle from the water and pointed it at an angle to shore. LeClaire nodded and stretched his paddle out, changing the direction of the canoe. Chris turned back and watched for the flash of the cross on the water. There was nothing except water as far as his eyes could see.

There ahead, however, just past the tall waves, was the mouth of an inlet to the cove called Mastigon. As they paddled closer, the waves slapped and splashed against the birchbark canoe, bouncing them in all directions. Bobbing up and down, the canoe rode the waves into the inlet, which led to the mouth of a calm lake.

The lake was big and round, and everywhere Nick and Chris looked they could see swampy marshes, undergrowth, and dead trees dangling over the water's edge. Lake grass and seaweed rubbed against the bottom of the canoe, sounding like fingernails scratching on a blackboard.

Meggie turned to the boys. "Mastigon means marshy lake. The sun will soon be gone into the west. It is best we rest here."

Chris thought that this wasn't the type of place he would pick to camp for the night. It looked like a swamp. But LeClaire soon found a small clearing along the shore where an area had been cleared from its tangle of weeds and deadwood. Directing the canoe into shallow water, he hopped out into waist deep weeds and water. Pushing the canoe forward through the water, he brought them close to shore.

Nick could see the grasses and reeds growing thick in the water below them. I sure wouldn't want to swim in this mess, thought Nick.

Meggie pulled in her paddle. Taking her moccasins off, she picked up the bundle she had brought from the cabin. When LeClaire brought the canoe to a stop, Meggie stepped into shallow water that was only knee deep.

"Take all you can carry and bring it to shore," she demanded.

Chris and Nick slipped off their moccasins and picked up their paddles and the other bundles. Chris slung his canteen across his shoulders and watched as Nick crawled out of the canoe. Sliding off the side, Nick dropped into the cool water and whined, "Oh, Yuck! This stuff feels slimy."

"Hurry up, Nick, I'm waiting. And watch out for snakes!" Chris teased.

Nick's eyes got as big as an owl's. He splashed through the water up to the shore as quickly as he could. Chris laughed as he slid into the water from the canoe. "That got ya moving, didn't it!" he laughed.

Not realizing his canteen had caught on the edge of the canoe, Chris started to wade away. The canteen pulled him tight, yanking him backward, off his feet and into the water.

Splash!

Nick and Meggie laughed as Chris sat waist deep in the muck and weeds. LeClaire offered his hand to help Chris.

"No thanks, I don't need your help!" he snapped. Dripping wet, Chris waded to shore, wringing out his shirt and dragging his canteen and paddle.

"I thought a snake got ya, Chris," joked Nick.

"Why don't you be quiet?" jeered Chris.

Meggie handed Nicholas her paddle and bag and waded back into the water to help LeClaire bring the canoe to shore. Once on shore, they carefully turned the canoe over. "We must move the canoe into the woods and away from the water so Le Diable Rouge will find no sign."

LeClaire took the paddles and walked into the wooded area surrounding the clearing. He was not gone long when he returned with empty hands.

"I found a place for a camp. It is big enough for the canoe. Come."

Meggie pulled her knife from her belt and walked into the woods, returning with a tree branch in her hand. Handing the branch to

Nicholas, she asked, "Do you know how to cover our trail?"

"Cover our trail?" Nick repeated.

"You must walk behind us. Drag the branch and wipe our footprints from the earth. We must leave no sign that we have left the water."

Nick smiled, "I can do that. I've seen that done in the movies."

Meggie and LeClaire stood at either end of the canoe and lifted it high into the air. Meggie got under the canoe first and balanced it on her head and shoulders. LeClaire then did the same.

"Wow! They must be strong," Chris said as he carried the paddles and Meggie's bag. Nick walked behind, dragging the long branch along the trail, being careful to erase all footprints they left along the shore.

Walking into the woods and over a knoll, they saw the perfect place LeClaire had found, where they could watch the mouth of the lake and still be safe from view.

Meggie and LeClaire lowered the canoe onto its side and then stuck a paddle in the ground to keep the canoe balanced and to prevent its rolling over. Chris piled the rest of the paddles against a tree, and Nick tossed his branch into the woods.

"We gather wood for fire now," said Meggie.

Chris, who was dripping wet, thought this was a good idea. He would do anything for some warm, dry clothes right now. Chris, Nick, and Meggie searched the area for dry dead wood and moss. Turning to the lake, Chris tried to imagine what this place would look like with a city and houses around it. Mastigon—Mastigon—Muskegon! This place is Muskegon Lake! he thought to himself.

Muskegon was a city not far from Grand Haven. It had a beautiful harbor, a channel, and a lighthouse. Wow, Muskegon—marshy waters—I get it! Chris stared at the primitive lake, amazed at the thought of traveling back in time before cities, factories, and cars.

While looking out over the lake, Christopher saw a shadow near the mouth of the lake. Ducking into the brush, he watched as a canoe with two figures bobbed up and down through the inlet and into the lake. It was McDougal and Grey Eyes.

"We will not have a fire tonight," whispered a low voice. It was Meggie with Nicholas, their arms full of wood, crouching down in the underbrush. They watched as the Devil and his friend passed by.

Good, thought Nick, who was glad he had covered their trail. They haven't seen where we left the water.

Returning to the canoe, they found LeClaire had already opened the bundles of food that Meggie had brought.

"Voilà, bon appetit, mon amis," (Good eating, my friends) said LeClaire, who already had a mouthful of food. "LeClaire, we saw McDougal and Grey Eyes," whispered Nick.

"Oui, I see also. They passed by on their way to the other side of the cove. They did not see us, but they know we are here."

"Do they smell us, LeClaire?" asked Nick.

"Oui, they may smell us, Little Fawn."

"Do not worry," said Meggie, looking at the boys. "We have good food to eat. We are safe, and we have our canoe to sleep under. We have all we need," Meggie smiled at Chris and Nick and laid her armload of wood on the ground.

Nick piled his wood quietly on the ground beside Meggie's. "Yeah, and if those guys come up here, we can throw wood at them."

Yeah, right, thought Chris. Chris wished he had never left the beach that morning. Right now he could be home in dry clothes, eating supper and maybe going out for an ice cream cone.

All four sat down beside the open bundles and ate dried meat and berries.

"This stuff isn't too bad. What is it?" inquired Nick.

"It's pemmican, made from dried venison or buffalo and mixed with wild nuts, dried berries, and grease. This is a meal voyageurs eat, because it is good and will last many moons without getting worms."

"Worms?" Nick scrunched up his face.

"*Oui*," rejoined LeClaire. "Worms no good. They squiggle around in your stomach. Make you sick."

Chris entered into the fun and wiggled his fingers in Nicholas' face.

"If we had a fire, LeClaire would find us a big fat turtle to cook. I make good turtle soup," Meggie said proudly.

Nick, reminded about turtles, reached deep into his pocket. The lump proved his warrior was still there, safe and watching over them.

LeClaire lifted his head and closed his eyes, breathing deep. Looking over to Nicholas, he asked, "Do you smell?"

Nick quickly closed his eyes. Yes, there it was—the smell of burning wood and hot grease.

Chris laughed, "Nick, do you smell? Yeah. You smell bad!"

"Chris, be quiet." Nick got up and stood close behind a tree, looking out over the lake. Directly across the cove was a ribbon of smoke coming from the shore. It was McDougal and Grey Eyes. They had pitched camp across the lake and were getting ready to eat.

"Do you think they really know we are here?" asked Nick quietly.

"They know," answered LeClaire. "This is the only safe harbor to spend the night. They have read our tracks in the sand at Gabagouache. They know there are two boys now, plus Madame and myself. They will wait and watch. Two boys would bring much silver to their pockets." LeClaire stood guard, looking out over the lake as the boys returned to the tilted canoe. "Eat now," said Meggie, "we will sleep, then leave while it is still dark—too dark for the Devil to see us."

Chris and Nick ate their fill of the dried meat and berries. It tasted like a health food snack their mother might buy at a store. When they were finished, Meggie made pillows out of the sacks and laid them under the canoe for the boys to sleep on. "This is a good place to sleep. The canoe will keep you warm and dry and the animals of the woods will not bother you here."

Chris's clothes were almost dry. It had been a long day. The two boys crawled under the tipped canoe and soon fell asleep.

It seemed they had been asleep only minutes when a sound, like thunder, echoed through the woods. Nicholas awoke, barely remembering where he was. Hearing the loud sound again, he felt very much afraid.

Chris crawled out first from under the canoe and stood silently, listening. The woods were dark and stars had come out, filling the night sky. There, standing by the tree, Chris could see the shadowy forms of Meggie and LeClaire watching out over the lake.

Crawling from under the canoe, Nick stood beside Chris and whispered, "What was that?"

"I don't—" Again the blast cut the darkness and made the boys shiver.

Chris and Nick quickly joined Meggie and LeClaire. They could see a huge fire burning in the distance, sending sparks high into the air. Its orange and red flames licked at the sky, and there, dancing around the fire, were two shadowy figures. It was McDougal and Grey Eyes.

Once more the blast was heard. McDougal was shooting his rifle into the air. The two devils yelled and laughed, their dancing forms highlighted by the fire.

"It is white man's milk that makes them act like Devils," said Meggie, as she slipped her arm around Nicholas's shoulder. "Do not be afraid of men like these. They are ignorant. We are smart. We know what we must do. These Devils will still be sleeping off the white man's milk when we will be almost to the Ile de Michilimackinac"

"Sleep now," whispered LeClaire to Chris. "I will need your strength in the canoe when we leave."

Chris and Nick returned to the upturned canoe and crawled under, finding sleep once again.

The moon, clear and bright, was low in the sky the next time Chris and Nick awoke. The fire of the renegades had burned down until only the orange glow of the coals could be seen across the cove.

Meggie and LeClaire had already carried the paddles and bundles down to the lake. It was time to go.

"*Bonjour, mon amis*, it is time to awake," called Meggie sweetly.

Time to go? thought Chris. It's the middle of the night.

Chris and Nick crawled from under the canoe as Meggie and LeClaire hoisted it high into the air over their heads.

Nick found a soft spot of moss and rolled himself into a ball and started to go back to sleep.

"Come on, Nick. I think they are going to leave us if we don't get going."

Meggie and LeClaire waded into the cold, black water and silently lowered the canoe. By the time the boys found their way down the knoll, Meggie was already in the canoe, waiting to go.

LeClaire waded back to the beach, lifted Nicholas onto his shoulder, and carried him out to the canoe. Then he returned for Chris who had already started wading toward the others.

"It's OK, LeClaire, I can take it."

"I will carry you. It is not good if you should get sick from the cold water. I need you to paddle."

"Come on LeCl—," Christopher started to say as LeClaire stooped down and picked him up and threw him over his shoulder like a sack of trade goods.

Nicholas laughed to himself, seeing how LeClaire had no trouble picking up his big brother.

When all was settled, LeClaire directed the canoe into open water. Pushing off, he crawled into the back and began paddling. They were on their way.

Silently, Meggie dipped her paddle into the black water, never raising it above the water. She paddled, making no sound. The weeds brushed against the bottom of the canoe. Nick hoped Red

Devil and Grey Eyes were fast asleep and would not hear them making their escape.

As they approached the mouth of the inlet, Chris and Nick also began paddling silently, like Meggie, never bringing their paddles out of the water. The water at the mouth of the inlet was not as choppy as it had been the day before. The canoe cut smoothly across the waves, and soon they cleared the land and once again entered Lake Michigan.

Safely away from the inlet, LeClaire began to sing a song in French. His low voice carried the tune to Madame La Framboise, who answered by repeating what he sang. It was a happy song, and the paddles cut through the water keeping pace with the music.

Nick remembered hearing stories from his mother about how voyageurs would sing while they paddled. It helped them pass the time and to keep their strokes in rhythm. Nick thought it must have also reminded them of their homes in France.

Nick felt like a real voyageur, out on Lake Michigan in a birchbark canoe, paddling to French songs. The moon's reflection danced across the open water and only shadows of the land could be seen mixing with tall, white hills of sand. He wondered how his parents were and knew they would be worried. Too bad, he thought, he couldn't call them on the phone just to let them know he and Chris were OK.

Soon, on the horizon, through the woods above the sand dunes, a faint shadow of pink like the inside of a shell, could be seen in the sky. The sun was rising. The sky began to grow lighter, and bright streaks of light cut the darkness.

LeClaire called out to Meggie in French and handed her the tobacco pouch. Steadying the canoe, Meggie stood and again scattered torn twists of tobacco to the four directions. She raised her hands, singing her beautiful song just as the sun peeked over the white dunes.

Chris and Nick both shivered. The sight was beautiful. It was real, not like something from a movie. Here was a real Métis, asking nature for a safe crossing on the great Lake of Michigan.

Deep down inside both boys knew everything would be all right with the help of their two friends. It was as it should be, and all was right with the world, even though Christopher's stomach growled from not having any breakfast.

Chapter 8
L'Arbre Croche

The little crew continued their journey along the shore as the sun climbed high into the sky. The bright warm sun showed its face on the water and the warmth felt good. It made Chris want to stretch, like a big cat.

As the sun rose higher, so did the waves, bouncing the canoe up and slapping it down, splashing them with water.

"The waves grow big because the sun warms the air," said LeClaire. "That is why it is good to paddle before the sun wakes up."

Chris remembered his mother telling stories about voyageurs starting their journey at three in the morning when they traveled the big lakes. He always thought it sounded dangerous to paddle at night, but now he understood that it was safer.

The four had been paddling along the coast for over an hour when Nicholas asked, "Can we take a pipe? I'm tired."

LeClaire steadied the canoe with his big paddle and the boys leaned back to rest. They all watched along the shore while they rested, looking for any sign of their enemies.

"LeClaire," asked Nick. "Why do you and Madame have such long paddles while Chris and mine are so short?"

"*Très bien*, (very good) that is a good question. My paddle is for the *gvenil* (goo-ver-ni), to reach out and steer the canoe. The *gvenil* stands in the back of the birchbark. Madame's paddle is for the *avant* (a-vont), who watches the water from the front of the canoe. At times the *avant* helps to steer the canoe also. You are *milieu* (mil-you), middle men. You provide the power. You have short paddles to push the water."

"That makes sense—the right paddle to fit the right job," agreed Nick.

"Do you hurt?" asked LeClaire as he passed the boys the tin of bear grease.

Chris and Nick, holding their breath, plunged their fingers deep into the goo, and rubbed it into their hands. "My stomach hurts too," said Chris. "I'm hungry."

Meggie reached into her bag and pulled out two sticks of dried meat that looked like beef jerky. "Here, this will help your belly. It is dried moose meat. LeClaire traded for this last season in Upper Canada."

Chris and Nick bit down hard on their moose sticks and chewed and chewed. It tasted dry and tough, but it soon filled their stomachs."That stuff's not bad," said Nick.

"Yeah," said Chris, "if you don't get bear grease from your hands on it. Yuck!" Meggie and LeClaire laughed.

"Meggie," said LeClaire, "show the boys how to paddle so they do not tire so easily. Madame will show you a special stroke."

The boys chewed their moose sticks as they listened to Meggie. She explained to them how to paddle every other stroke. Then they could paddle, and rest, paddle and rest.

"That sounds simple. I like the resting part best," said Nick.

Soon they were on their way once again. The sun shone high in the sky and their stomachs were full. The boys tried the new paddling stroke and it worked just fine.

All morning they paddled, cutting across the waves, moving farther and farther away from Grand Haven, the cove of Mastigon, and hopefully, the two Devils. LeClaire watched for signs of their enemies as he paddled. McDougal and Grey Eyes were probably just waking up from their wild party and only now were wondering where they were and watching for them.

The "pipes" along the trip were never long enough to suit Chris and Nick. And it was hard being on their knees, cramped in one position for such a long time. Their hands and muscles ached and the boys could think of nothing except getting to Mackinac Island.

LeClaire helped pass the time by singing many different French songs.

The boys watched Meggie and became better paddlers. They learned not to stretch the paddle out too far, because it made the arms tired. She told them not to dig the paddle into the water too deeply, because to paddle lightly helped the canoe move faster and saved the paddler's strength. Sit tight to the edge, she had reminded them, for more control. And above all, don't slam your thumb between the side of the canoe and the paddle. Chris had already tried that and didn't like it.

Nicholas did his best to keep paddling, but often found it hard not to let his mind wander. After all, he was on a great adventure—an adventure that spanned over two hundred years.

"Meggie," asked Nick, "do you believe people can travel back in time?"

Meggie thought for a moment and turned to look at Nicholas.

"Nick, you goofball," said Chris, "why did you ask her that? She's going to think we're crazy."

"*Oui*," said Meggie, "I believe that with the great spirit all things are possible. There are many stories I have heard told by the *conteur*, the French storyteller. He tells tales about French men and women who have traveled back in time. They go for a reason—to help the future, to learn about people, or even to save lives. The stories of the *midewiwin* (Indian medicine men) and the old grandfathers within the lodges tell of warriors traveling through time on the back of a great turtle spirit."

Nick looked at Christopher, "A great turtle spirit?" said Nick. They both thought of the turtle warrior rock Nick had picked up on the top of the dune in Grand Haven.

"There are holy people, both men and women that travel through time, too, changing their shapes to animals and then back to people again. They are special to all living beings. That is why the Odawa give thanks to the animals we hunt. We thank the manitous for coming to us. We pray they will forgive us for taking their lives, in case they may be a holy person," continued Meggie.

"Wow! You don't think this is weird?" asked Chris.

"Do you, Little Fawn, feel you have traveled to us through time?"

Nick thought for a minute and nodded his head "yes."

"And do you also believe this?" she asked Christopher.

"I think something really strange has happened to us," said Chris. We used to live in a town called Grand Haven. Now there's nothing there except Gabagouache, the Indian settlement. We have been to Muskegon."

"You mean Mastigon, " said Meggie.

"Well, yeah, but where we are from, it's called Muskegon. There's a big city there, bigger than Grand Haven. Not all those weeds and marshes.

All along the lake there are towns and cities. We haven't seen an airplane since we got here."

"An air-e-o-plan? What is this?" asked LeClaire.

"An airplane, LeClaire. It flies in the air and carries people," explained Chris.

"The great turtle spirit, Madame."

"No, an airplane. It's a machine with a motor."

"A motor like a boat. I see," said LeClaire.

"You said you have been to the Ile de Michilimackinac. Is that true?" asked Meggie. "And if so, in your time, tell me how it is."

"Oh, Mackinac Island is great!" said Nick. "It's real neat. They have all these old houses and shops that line the streets. And there is a great big white stone fort."

"*Oui*, the fort is made of stone, so it will last a long time. Is the church of Saint Anne still there? The Church is on the street before the fort. Does it still stand?"

"Yeah," said Nick. "Chris, remember walking past that church with Dad? It was down past all those houses and hotels. It's a big white church with those bells that ring real loud."

"A big white church? With bells? asked Meggie. "The Saint Anne is small, and made like an Indian lodge. It became big? This is good!"

"Did the British leave the island? Are the American soldiers there in your time?"

"Wow! I don't believe this," said Chris. "You think the British are still at the fort? What year are we in, anyway?"

Meggie shrugged her shoulders, "The year I do not know."

"There was a great war to the east," said LeClaire. "The King named George made war with his colonies. That was twenty seasons ago. I was young and lived with my mama at Port Royal. It was during the war that my papa, the African prince, was killed trying to protect his master. I will never forget hearing about this great war."

Nick scrunched up his face and looked at Chris. "The Revolutionary War, Nick. He's talking about the Revolutionary War! Let's see— 1776 and twenty years would make this 1796. Nick, we're in 1796!"

Chris was so excited that he jumped up and faced LeClaire. "LeClaire, it's 1796, the year the Americans took over the Northwest Territories from the British. I learned about all this in my Michigan history class at school!"

LeClaire, surprised at Chris's action, just smiled a big grin and steadied the canoe. "Sit down, boy. You will tip us over," boomed LeClaire.

Chris quickly sat on the floor of the canoe. "Nick, did you hear that? 1796!"

Nick had heard all right, and he wasn't sure he liked it. This was the first time Nick had ever been away from home. And now, being two hundred years away from home was scary. How were they ever going to get back? What would their parents think of them being two hundred years early for dinner?

Nick paddled quietly as he thought about all this. He could feel tears starting to burn his eyes. What if they could never get home again?

"Nick, are you all right?" Chris whispered.

Nick gulped hard and wiped the tears from his eyes on the sleeve of his shirt. "I'm OK, I guess."

Meggie smiled at Nicholas. "Do not worry. The great spirit is mighty and wonderful. He will help you find your answers. The Black Robe Jesuit priest, when he comes to the Ile d e

Michilimackinac, will help you find your way home. He is a good man. He is educated in France. He will know what to do."

"He will?" asked Nick.

"See Nick, we're OK. The Black Robe will help us get back. Just don't worry. Just think about how many kids get to see 1796? We're special!"

Nick thought for a moment and knew Chris was probably right. Reaching to his pocket, he patted the turtle warrior rock. Help us, turtle warrior, Nick thought to himself. That turtle warrior rock must be magical.

The tiny crew paddled on. Chris and Nick watched the shoreline, looking for anything familiar. There was nothing except more sand, dunes, woods, and grass. Chris had traveled along Lake Michigan hundreds of times, but only by car. The shoreline was different now, and nothing looked the same. LeClaire, every so often, would stop paddling and steady the canoe, searching the horizon for any sign of McDougal and Grey Eyes. He knew they were out there, somewhere, looking for them.

As the afternoon wore on, clouds began to gather in the sky. Nicholas watched as the first clouds, white fluffy ones, gathered. They looked like marshmallow men. Soon grey ones gathered and the sky darkened. LeClaire and Meggie paddled faster. There was no rest now as the crew pushed on across the water.

It wasn't long before Nicholas could see drops of water on the back of Meggie's shoulders as light sprinkles of rain began to fall. A cool breeze picked up, and waves blew across the water. The breeze grew sharp and cold and chilled Nicholas through and through.

"Madame," said LeClaire, "we sleep tonight at *L'Arbre Croche* (The Crooked Tree)."

Meggie nodded her head "yes" as she continued to paddle at a steady pace, not wanting to slow their escape from the oncoming storm.

The clouds grew darker, blocking out the sun. Day turned to night. Waves swept across the lake, pushing the canoe close to land.

"*Gim me one*," called Meggie. "That means 'rainy weather' in Odawa."

"Gim me one. Hey, that's funny," said Chris. "Meggie, how about, 'don't gimme one.' That means no rainy weather in American."

"Are we going to stop and go ashore?" Nick called above the wind and rain.

"Not here," answered LeClaire, "but soon."

The rain fell harder and harder. Puddles of water gathered around their feet and knees. Meggie handed Nicholas two handfuls of sheep's wool from her bag.

"Soak the water from the canoe," she instructed.

Nick began soaking up water and wringing it into the lake. The wool was like a sponge. It sucked up the water, helping to keep the canoe dry. As soon as Nick thought he had all the water, the rain would fill the canoe bottom again.

The rain hit hard across their backs and arms. Nick had never heard of being out on the water when there was a storm, especially in a canoe! The canoe rose high on the waves and water sloshed into it as the waves slapped at its sides. Nick was afraid.

Christopher kept paddling as fast as he could with the pace that Meggie set. His arms and hands ached, but it was better to paddle fast than to have to swim in the cold lake.

LeClaire was even paddling with his long paddle. He had pulled on a thick, blue wool shirt to keep him warm. As he worked hard paddling, a steamy mist rose from his shoulders. The heat of his body and the cold rain left a vapor trail as the canoe moved forward.

Soon the rain lightened, and although the sprinkling continued, the clouds did not look so angry. The canoe changed direction. There under the mist along the shore lay an inlet. The mouth of the inlet was wider than at Mastigon, and the waves were not as hard to cross. The wind blew from behind, helping them direct the fragile vessel into a horseshoe-shaped harbor. Once into the harbor, Nicholas heard a sound that he thought was thunder. Then, remembering the sound of McDougal's gun, he realized the thunder was manmade. The boys looked at each other, wondering if it was the two Devils.

As they came closer to shore, Nicholas could see men shooting their rifles into the air and waving their arms in greeting. Along the shore, lead-colored smoke rose from a long row of Indian lodges that lined the shore of the lake. There were lots of them. This must be the Indian town, L'Arbre Croche, Nick thought to himself.

Exhausted, Chris pulled his paddle into the canoe. He laid his head against the side of the canoe, happy to be able to rest.

"They welcome us," LeClaire called to the boys. "These are Madame's people. They will let us rest here for the night."

Nick and Chris were glad to see the friendly faces of the people standing along the shore. The rain, still falling gently, was getting even colder. Nicholas's teeth began to chatter as he pulled the cold wet cloth of his shirt away from his skin.

LeClaire jumped into the cold, grey water, guiding the canoe to shore. Men from the village waded out to help LeClaire, bringing the canoe up onto the sand.

Two men put their arms together and made a seat for Madame. Together they carried her from the canoe onto the shore. Once there, women from the village gathered around Meggie, wrapping her in blankets and greeting her with hugs.

Another man came out into the water and lifted Nicholas out of the canoe. Placing Nicholas high on his shoulders, the man waded to shore through waist-deep water. Looking back, Nicholas could see Christopher shake his head as a man tried to help him out of the canoe.

LeClaire called to the man, giving him instructions on how to handle the stubborn boy. The man grabbed Chris's legs and pulled him from the canoe onto his shoulders.

Nick laughed as he watched Chris come ashore. Chris looked like a big sack of potatoes thrown across the man's shoulder.

"They don't get it," said Chris as the man dropped him on the shore. "I can walk like the rest of the men. Why does everyone want to carry me like a baby?"

The Indian women gathered around the boys with warm dry blankets, wrapping them from head to foot. Meggie smiled and spoke with the women in a language that neither Chris nor Nick had heard before. It wasn't French, it was different. This must be the way Indians speak, Nick thought.

Once the boys were wrapped in warm blankets, the group entered a large, shaggy-looking house that was long and round on each end. Inside two fires blazed. The house, which was very neat, was warm and comfortable. Woven mats covered the dirt floor and looked like a colorful carpet. Big fur bundles, soft and warm, lay folded against the wall. Little children ran back and forth, excited to see they had company.

Meggie motioned for the boys to sit near the first fire to warm themselves. Soon LeClaire entered, talking a mixture of French and Indian. It was funny how Nicholas could now tell if LeClaire was talking French. The French words sounded like they came from the nose and throat. Indian words, however, were soft and gentle.

The men all stood around the second fire at the far end of the lodge. As their clothes began to dry, their shirts steamed. A mist rose high into the air and disappeared, up the smoke hole in the roof. Chris watched and poked Nick to see the unusual sight. "They look like they're on fire," whispered Chris.

LeClaire soon pulled off his soaked shirt, wrapped himself in a warm blanket, and began to smoke a pipe with the Indian men. Meggie, who had disappeared, soon returned wrapped in an outfit made of a long blanket, like a big robe, and sat beside the boys.

Chris and Nick shivered from their wet clothes and wished they could change also. LeClaire, who had kept an eye on the boys, brought them two heavy woolen shirts made from blankets. "Take off wet clothes and put these on."

Nick and Chris pulled off their soggy shirts. Chris began to wring his shirt out when LeClaire quickly grabbed it from his hands.

"Chris," said Nick, "don't do that in the house. I don't think these ladies would be too happy if you got their mats all wet."

An Indian woman came over quickly. She gave Christopher a stern look and took the shirt from LeClaire and hung it to dry by the fire. Two young Indian girls came near the fire and watched them closely. The girls giggled and smiled and spoke quietly to each other. Soon they reached out and snatched up Nicholas's wet shirt and spread it to dry over a frame at the back of the lodge. The girls returned to the fire to sit close to the boys.

An older woman walked by, tussling Chris's hair, saying "*Qui-nage Che-mok-e-mon,*" to the girls.

"Hey, watch it," said Chris as he pulled away from her. "What'd she say, Meggie?"

Meggie leaned over to the boys and whispered, "I think the grandmother believes you would make good husbands for her granddaughters. She called you 'pretty white men.'"

"No way, yuck," said Nick. "I'm only eight. And I'm not pretty!"

"That's for sure," said Chris. "And I don't think she wants a twelve-year-old husband for her granddaughter, either."

Meggie laughed. "Twelve years is a good age for marriage."

Soon, one of the girls moved closer to Nicholas and stared directly into his face.

"Meggie!" called Nick in a panic. LeClaire, who was watching from the other fire, laughed loudly and directed the men's attention to what was happening.

The young girl reached out with her finger and placed it on Nicholas's freckles, one at a time. "Hey, cut it out," Nick shrugged away.

"Take it easy, little brother," said Chris, enjoying the joke. "She thinks you're cute!"

Nick stood quickly and moved to the other side of the fire beside Meggie. Meggie, who was sipping a bowl of soup, handed Nicholas her bowl. The girl who had tried to count Nicholas's freckles handed Christopher a bowl, which he quickly drank.

"This soup is good," said Chris. "A lot better than moose on a stick with bear grease!" Chris and Nick each had a second bowl and soon felt warm, dry, and sleepy.

Two little children, not more than a year old, came near the fire to watch the strangers. The tiny children, who looked like twins, were entirely naked. They soon scooted up beside Nick and snuggled close.

"Hey, don't these kids wear diapers?" Nick asked.

"I'm glad they are sitting with you," Chris added. The boys laughed and Nick tried to move away.

Meggie chatted with the women as she warmed herself beside the fire. She spoke to them of their adventures with McDougal and Grey Eyes.

Chris and Nick listened as the women made sounds of oh's and ah's and looked at the boys with amazement.

"I bet she is telling them that we are from outer space or something," said Chris.

"Yeah," said Nick. "I hope they don't decide they don't like time travelers."

One of the young girls pulled down a big fur robe from the side of the lodge wall and spread it out. She patted the robe and called to Chris.

"It is good you should rest now," said Meggie. "You both were good voyageurs today."

"I guess I am pretty tired," said Chris, as he crawled over to the robe on all fours and plopped down in the middle. The young girl sat at the fire in Chris's place and turned to watch Chris, who was ignoring her.

"Oh, Chris," teased Nick, "I think you have a girlfriend." Chris rolled over and wrapped up tightly in his fur robe. Nick laughed as he watched the pretty Indian girl stare at Chris.

Soon Nick could hear Christopher gently snoring. I don't believe it, Nick thought to himself. How does he rate? I'm tired too! Nick crawled over to the fur robe where Chris lay sound asleep and gave him a poke. "Chris, move over. I want to lie down, too." Soon the second girl brought Nicholas a fur robe. She smiled at Nick and laid the robe on the mat beside Christopher.

I don't care, Nick thought, I just want to rest. Nick cuddled up beside Chris, and soon they were both fast asleep.

Chapter 9

The Feast

When Nick awoke, he and Christopher were alone in the bark-covered lodge. The fire, which burned low, glowed with an eerie orange light in the dimly-lit room.

"Chris, wake up."

"Leave me alone, I'm tired," grunted Chris. "I want to sleep some more."

"Chris, everyone's gone. We're all alone."

"They're probably sleeping. Leave me alone," urged Chris.

Nick unrolled from his fur robe, stood by the glow of the fire, and looked around. He could see the bundles Meggie had brought with her in the canoe lying open on mats to dry.

Yuck! thought Nick. I hope we don't have to eat pemmican again tonight. Nick reached down among the things drying and picked out a piece of moose meat which he began to chew while wondering where everyone had gone.

At that moment, Nicholas heard voices coming from outside the lodge. Checking the lodge walls, he looked for a door. He soon spied a large blue blanket covering a hole in the wall. Quietly lifting the edge, he peeked out. There, not far from the opening, sat Meggie on a red blanket. Spread before her were lots of small objects like pins, haircombs, mirrors, earrings, and colorful beads. Several Indian women stood behind Meggie, admiring the many bright and useful items. The men, however, stood to the side, smoking their pipes and listening to LeClaire as he spoke.

Nick pulled the blanket back farther and walked out into the cool, rain-washed sunlight. The dark clouds that had once filled the sky were now gone and the late afternoon sun shone bright.

"*Me no ki she gut*," Meggie called to Nick as she spied him coming from the lodge.

Nick looked at Meggie. She must be speaking Algonquin, he thought. Nick remembered his mother telling him about how different Indian tribes spoke different languages. These people, the Odawa, spoke the Algonquin language.

Meggie motioned for Nicholas to join her on the blanket. "I said, 'It is a nice day. The clouds and rain are gone.'"

"Yeah, it is a nice day," said Nick as he looked around. "What's LeClaire doing?"

"He tells the men our tale, and how we have need of their help," she whispered to Nick. "These things before me are trade goods. I packed them when we made ready for our escape. LeClaire tells the men there will be much more if they help us." Nick now understood. These things were the price Meggie would pay for their safety.

"Meggie, I thought these people were your family. Wouldn't they just help you anyway?"

"*Oui*, Little Fawn, they will help LeClaire and me, but you and your brother are Americans— Americans who have traveled through time. They fear you bring them *motchi manitou*, bad luck.

"You must understand, the Odawa depend upon a good hunt for food and a good trading season for bullets, kettles, and traps. If the hunt is bad because they have offended the *manitos*, their families will suffer," Meggie explained.

"It is good that everyone knows of Le Diable Rouge. He has cheated them many times. The Red Devil has told my people if they do not trade with him, he will send the Americans to destroy their villages. Do you understand why they fear you and your brother?"

Nick nodded his head "yes." That McDougal's a real jerk, he thought.

Just then, Chris pulled back the blanket door of the lodge and walked out into the sunlight. Chris now had on his own shirt, which had dried beside the fire.

"Chris, come here and check out this stuff," called Nick. Chris joined him at the blanket, looking over the many things Meggie had brought to trade. Nick told Chris everything that was going on and how LeClaire was bartering for their safety.

Chris watched the faces of the men as they spoke. "They look nervous to me. I don't know if they are going to help us," he whispered.

"They must help us," said Meggie. "The evening will soon be here. McDougal and Grey Eyes will not be far away."

Meggie picked up a long string of beads and held them high in the air, showing them off to the women. The women ran their hands over the smooth, colorful beads and talked among themselves with great smiles upon their faces.

These Indian people, Nick thought, are not like the Indians in the movies. They don't all look the same. Some are round, some are thin, some tall, and some short. There are even some with very light skin, and others who are tan and dark. The women and girls all have long dark hair, but some pull it back with bits of ribbon or pieces torn from a blanket. Others have beaded bands or braids around their heads.

The hair of the men is different also. Some have long hair and others have short. Some wear feathers and others red knitted caps. The Indians, Nick thought, were supposed to all look alike with long black hair and bows and arrows. These people were just like everyone else. They fixed their hair and dressed in whatever way they liked.

Nick noticed some of the women decorated their dresses the way Meggie did, with lots of beads and ribbons. Others were wearing very plain dresses with lots of necklaces. There were even women with black paint on their faces. They stood quietly off by themselves and did not talk with the rest.

The men wore a mixture of clothing, too. Some had shirts like LeClaire's, and some had no shirts at all. Some wore pants that tied at the knees, and some wore a funny-looking cloth, like a diaper. There was even one old man with a red uniform coat and a big silver medal hanging from his neck.

One thing everyone did seem to have, however, was his or her own blanket, either tied around the waist or shoulders or lying in a heap around his or her feet. And everyone had moccasins, too, like the ones Meggie had given him! What a colorful, interesting group of people! I hope I never forget how these people look, thought Nick, especially after I go back to my own time.

Patting his pants, Nick could feel his turtle rock snug and safe. Reaching into his pocket, he pulled out the rock and held it up to the sunlight, checking all its angles. Yep, that's a turtle warrior, all right. I hope its magic will help get us back home, he said to himself.

Just then, the old Indian with the red uniform coat looked at Nicholas and called out to him.

"Nick," said Chris, "I think that man is talking to you."

Nick looked around and noticed all the Indians were now staring at him. "What? What's the matter?" asked Nick. Meggie walked to Nick's side as the old Indian called to him even louder.

"*Kitchi Mishinemackinong* (Great Turtle).

"Little Fawn," asked Meggie, "where did you get this stone?"

"This? I found it in Grand Haven on the top of the sand dune. It's my turtle warrior rock!"

"*Oui*, it is a turtle stone. It looks like the sacred turtle, Kitchi Mishinemackinong. This is good. Your stone may help us."

The old man walked slowly toward Nicholas. His hair, long and grey with age, hung loose over his shoulders. Feathers, painted red, were tied in his hair and swung back and forth as he walked. In his hands he carried a long pipe, painted red, with four ribbons and a feather hanging from it.

"Meggie, Meggie, what does he want?" asked Nick fearfully.

The man looked very important. Everyone watched and listened as he spoke. Slowly he reached out his arms to Nicholas, holding the long pipe.

"He wants you to take the pipe and smoke," urged Meggie.

"Meggie!" Nick said with surprise.

"The old Chief offers you the peace pipe. This is a great honor."

Nick looked wide-eyed at Meggie. "I can't smoke that thing. My mom and dad would get real mad."

"Meggie, he's right," said Chris. "We don't smoke. It's not allowed. Our parents would be very upset with us."

LeClaire, having overheard the boys, stepped forward from the group of men. Standing between the old man and Nick, LeClaire spoke.

"Nicholas, you are part of something special because of this stone. You must obey."

"I'll do anything, but I can't smoke that pipe," said Nick in a stubborn manner.

LeClaire spoke with the old Indian, who did not understand why a boy so honored would not make smoke. Finally, however, the old man nodded his head "yes." He looked at Nicholas and smiled.

"*Très bien*," said Meggie. "LeClaire will stand in your place, but you both must be blessed by the smoke of the pipe this day."

LeClaire and the old man reached out their arms to each other, shaking arms as one would shake hands. The old man placed the pipe in a long leather bag decorated with feathers. Another man carried it to the Chief's lodge.

"Little Fawn, the Chief wants to look at the turtle stone," said Meggie.

The old man reached out his rough, shaky hands to Nicholas. Nick carefully placed the rock in his hands. The Chief smiled with delight and held it high above his head. Addressing his people, he spoke in a loud, excited voice.

"Nick," said Chris, "I don't understand this, do you? It's just a rock."

"I don't care. It's OK with me, just so they'll help us."

The old man carefully returned the turtle rock to Nicholas. Then he spoke in a gentle voice, all the while shaking his head up and down.

"Meggie, what's he saying?" asked Chris.

"The old Chief tells your brother he will always be safe in the village of *Wau-go-naw-ki-sa*, the Indian name for Crooked Tree. And he will protect him from the Red Devil and Grey Eyes. It is time now, however, to smoke from the pipe to bless you both." The old man turned and walked toward his lodge.

Wow, thought Chris, all this fuss over a dumb rock. Nick put his turtle warrior back in his pocket and followed the Chief. Nick was happy, because he always knew his rock was something special.

Chris, Meggie, and LeClaire followed closely behind Nick to the Chief's lodge, which stood near the center of the village. This lodge was bigger than most of the others and had three fires burning inside.

LeClaire, Meggie, Nick, and Chris were instructed to sit around the center fire beside the Chief. Soon others joined the group. The men seated themselves around the three fires. The women stood quietly behind the men.

The long red pipe was again brought to the old Chief, who unwrapped it carefully from its leather bag. Another bag with bright colored-beads on it was also opened. Inside was something that looked like chopped grass and weed clippings.

"This is *kinnic-kinic*," said Meggie, "Indian tobacco. It is a blend of many plants, and the bark of the red willow, a favorite of the Great Manitou."

The Chief filled the pipe and carefully lit it with a piece of wood from the fire. He drew long, hard puffs, and the pipe started to burn. Sweet smelling, purple-grey smoke began filling the air as the Chief puffed away.

"Yuck," said Nick," haven't they ever heard of a non-smoking section?"

The boys giggled. LeClaire gave them a cross look to make them be quiet, and Meggie jabbed Nick with her elbow.

Quietly the boys sat watching the old man as he stood and lifted the red pipe to the four sacred directions and began to speak.

"Meggie," whispered Nick, "what's he saying?"

Meggie leaned near the boys and spoke in a low voice. "The pipe is red because it is a color of strength and plenty. These four ribbons hanging on the stem are the four quarters of the universe. The black one is for the west, where thunder comes from. The white one stands for the north, where the great cleansing snow wind comes from.

The red ribbon is for the east, where the morning star lives. The yellow ribbon is for the south, where summer comes from to make the corn grow. These four directions all come from one good spirit. This feather is the symbol for that one. Now, we give thanks."

"Chris," whispered Nick, "this is like what Meggie did in the canoe with the twist of tobacco."

"Yeah, it's like an Indian prayer," said Chris.

The old Chief took another long puff, sat down, and passed the pipe to LeClaire. LeClaire, taking the pipe in both hands, puffed big plumes of smoke into the air and passed it to Meggie who did the same.

LeClaire then instructed the boys to rise to their knees and close their eyes. Soon both boys could smell the sweet burning *kinnic-kinic* all around them. Chris opened his eyes ever so slightly and could see LeClaire puffing plumes of smoke into the air, while Meggie fanned the smoke around them. Nicholas began feeling dizzy from all the smoke. He hoped it would soon be over.

Meggie reached out and signaled the boys to sit. They sat in their place beside the fire and the

Chief again spoke to his people. Chris and Nick could tell he was pleased.

The old Chief emptied the pipe into the fire and again wrapped it in its feather bag.

"*Très bien*," said Meggie, "*we-sin*, or as you say, we eat."

Eat! That was the best thing Chris had heard all day. Soon steaming bowls of soup were passed among the men. The women hurried back and forth around the lodge, talking quietly and serving them. There was dried fish, dried venison meat, fresh berries, dried berries, nuts, roots, pemmican, and green leafy stuff that looked like weeds but tasted sweet. All sorts of food, strange but good tasting, was offered to them.

Everyone dug into the great wooden bowls of food with their hands or ate off small pieces of bark. Dogs ran in and out of the lodge, gobbling the food that dropped to the mats.

The Chief had a special dog that sat quietly beside him while he ate. Whenever the Chief's hands were greasy, he wiped them across the dog's fur like a napkin. The dog didn't mind, but just kept licking his fur clean over and over.

Nick watched the old Chief in amazement, not believing what he was seeing. The Chief looked up at Nick and smiled. "*Mo-kaw-gee*, (dog)," he said and patted the dog lovingly.

"Wow, Nick," said Chris, "Mom wouldn't even let our dog in the house, let alone use him as a napkin. This is great!"

Meggie helped with the meal and ate with the women as they worked on the feast. The men sat around the fire, talking loudly, burping, laughing, picking their teeth with the tips of their hunting knives, and demanding more food when each bowl was empty.

"I wonder if the women always eat by themselves?" Nick asked Chris. "I bet Mom wouldn't like that."

"Nick, I think these women would rather eat by themselves, instead of watching the men burp, pick their teeth, and wipe their hands on dog fur."

Nick thought for a moment and decided that Chris was probably right.

Their stomachs full, the boys made their way through the group of happy people and left the feast, walking between the shaggy lodges to the beach. The lodges in the village were all built the same way, except some were big, like the Chief's, and some were small. All of them, however, had shaggy layers of bark covering the outside. The tops were covered with woven mats with smoke holes left open over each fire.

The sun was just beginning to go down, and the boys hurried to the beach to watch it set. The sun, looking like a great fireball, began to sink deep into Lake Michigan. The boys watched the sun from the mouth of the inlet at L'Arbre Croche (Crooked Tree). "Wow," said Chris, "this is great."

"I wish Mom and Dad were here to see all this, don't you Chris?"

"Yeah, but I kind of wish I was home watching it on TV, too. You know what I mean?"

The boys laughed and at the same time heard girls giggling. It was the two girls from the lodge. "Oh brother, I don't believe this. They followed us down here," said Chris.

Nick thought it was funny. Chris tried to ignore them. "Chris's got a girlfriend. Chris's got a girlfriend," chanted Nick in a whisper.

"You think that's funny, Nick? I think you've got one too!"

Nick turned and there, standing beside him, was the young girl who counted his freckles. She smiled sweetly at Nick.

The boys, trying to ignore the girls, silently watched the sun drop below the horizon. With all the excitement of the day, they had forgotten about McDougal and Grey Eyes. Somewhere out there, however, McDougal and Grey Eyes were thinking about them.

The boys soon returned to the Chief's lodge, the girls following close behind. Everyone from the lodge stood outside. The men were preparing to light a great fire. Everyone brought stacks of dried wood and piled it high in the fire circle. A burning torch, brought from the Chief's lodge, lit the fire. Soon flames of orange, yellow, and red leaped high into the evening air.

Two men with a large circle of wood covered tightly with an animal skin soon appeared. A young boy about Nick's age knelt down on the ground, balancing the circle against him. When the boy was ready, the two men pulled out long sticks with balls of leather on the end and began beating the skin.

"Nick, check this out," said Chris excitedly, "it's a drum!"

Several men gathered around the drum, each carrying his own padded drumstick. Once the beat was set, the men began to sing. The people of the village gathered and danced in a circle around the fire.

Meggie soon joined the watching boys. "The people dance to tell the stories of their hunts, the stories of the eagle and the turtle. To dance is a good thing. *'Gi neem nuck ko?'* Do you dance?" she asked Chris.

"No way, not me," he said and quickly walked away.

Nick watched and listened. The music followed the beat of the big drum. The men sang together, sometimes low and sometimes very high and loud.

The Odawa danced in their soft moccasin slippers. Puffs of dust rose from their feet as they danced around and around the fire. They hopped from one foot to the other. Some, opening their blankets wide, cast shadows that looked like great birds on the lodge walls.

Nick could see Chris trying to move closer to the drum, watching the men pounding out the rhythm and singing. One man, covered with sweat, handed Christopher his drumstick and moved away so that Chris could play.

Excitedly, Christopher stepped into his place and joined the musicians, following the beating rhythm. There, standing behind Christopher, Nick could see the young Indian girl watching and smiling.

"Look, Meggie, that girl keeps following Chris."

"She is *qui-nag* (pretty). They call her *Wau-wass kona*, Flower."

"That's neat. What's the other girl's name?"

"You mean the one that follows you? "They call her *Waugoshance*, Little Fox."

"Wow, Little Fox. I like that!" Nick said, smiling to himself.

The dance and the music continued for a long time. Late that evening after Chris and Nick had returned to their lodge, they could still hear the pounding heart of the Indian drum.

Chapter 10
Turtle Warrior

The next morning, when the boys awoke, the lodge was busy with life. Meggie and LeClaire sat beside the fire talking quietly. The women and children rushed back and forth, preparing for their day's work.

Nick rolled out of his fur robe and stretched. Chris, who was already awake, was outside washing for breakfast.

The sun was high in the morning sky when Nick went outside. It seemed nice to sleep in, he thought to himself. After drawing water from an animal skin, he scrubbed his face in a wooden bowl and tossed the water into the woods.

"Hurry up, Nick," called Chris, as he waited, "I want to eat." Chris entered the lodge and Nick soon followed.

"Chris, you always want to eat," said Nick.

The smoke hole above the fire pit let in only a little of the bright morning sun. If you didn't know better, you might think it was still dark outside. Maybe that's why everyone is outside most of the time, Nick thought.

The boys watched Meggie dish up two wooden bowls of something from a kettle. From a small bark box, she took two hard brown lumps and broke them into the bowls.

"Yuck, what's that?" asked Chris rudely.

"*Sagamity*, corn soup, with *ze-ze-baw-qua-donce*, candy. *Très bien* . You must hurry to eat, for we leave soon. Le Diable Rouge will catch up with us today if he did not sleep with the white man's milk last night."

The boys tasted their corn syrup, using a small piece of clam shell as a spoon. "*Sagamity*," repeated Chris, "not bad."

"Chris, this is good. That brown stuff tastes like maple syrup. It's like hot cereal."

The boys ate all they had in their bowls and asked for more. It was sweet and warm and felt good in their stomachs.

"Nicholas," said Meggie, when the boys had finished eating. "Where do you keep the turtle stone?"

Nick patted his pants pocket. "It's right here. Why?"

"It is a special stone that you possess. It needs to be kept safe."

Nick stood and pulled the turtle warrior rock from his pocket. "See, it's right here," and as Nicholas looked at the rock, he remembered the dream he had had the night before.

"Wow, I just remembered something," he said. "I had this weird dream last night. It was all about this rock and Indian people."

"Was the dream about the Odawa?" asked Meggie.

"Yeah, I think it was. I can remember the old Chief being there, wearing his red coat. He rode on the head of the turtle warrior."

Meggie stood quickly and ran from the lodge. She returned with the Chief and several older men, who sat down beside Nicholas.

"Little Fawn," said Meggie, "tell us your dream."

Nick tried to remember, and after awhile the dream became very clear. Meggie sat near Nicholas, repeating every word he spoke in Algonquin, so the Odawa would understand.

"In my dream," started Nick, "the turtle warrior rock sat beside me at a fire while I ate a great feast like we had last night. When all the food was gone, the dancers began to dance around the fire and play a drum. Then the turtle warrior moved and came to life."

After Meggie told the Chief all this, his eyes grew wide.

"The Chief was in my dream," Nick continued. "He danced with the turtle warrior around three fires. The turtle warrior grew bigger and bigger until he was bigger than any of the lodges in the village. No one was afraid of the turtle warrior. He was everyone's friend."

The old men around the fire listened to the story, smiling and nodding their heads in approval.

"In my dream it started to rain, and everyone was afraid. A big bird came down from the sky with lightning bolts and thunder in its claws. It was trying to put out the fires."

The old men listened with fearful looks on their faces.

"The turtle warrior wasn't afraid, it just grew bigger and bigger until it covered the whole village. Finally the big bird left and the rain stopped. The rain did not put out the fires.

"The turtle put all the Odawa people on its back with the three fires. And the Chief rode on the turtle's head, wearing his red coat."

The Chief sat tall and proud now among his friends.

"The turtle swam to Lake Michigan," Nick continued. "He swam and swam until he reached Mackinac Island, then he climbed ashore and fell asleep on the warm, sandy beach.

"Everyone was happy. They sang and danced around the three fires on the back of the great turtle. That was the end of my dream."

Soon crowds of people began coming into the lodge and the story was repeated over and over until everyone from the village had heard the wonderful dream. They all spoke among themselves, telling how proud they were to have a dreaming boy at their village.

"Chris, I don't believe this," said Nick. "My dream meant something to these people."

The old Chief who sat close to Nick asked Meggie if he could see the brave turtle warrior stone again.

Nick handed the rock to the Chief, who had tears in his eyes. The Chief stood before his people with the rock in his hand. He spoke with great emotion. The tears fell from his eyes and the people were quiet as they listened.

Meggie leaned toward the boys and told them the Chief was honored to hold the symbol of a great turtle warrior in his hands—the warrior who saved the three fires from the great thunder bird in your dream, the warrior who brought them to the Ile de Michilimackinac, where celebration takes place and where Americans will soon live.

"The Chief believes your dream is a message from the Great Manitou, who watches over his "people of the three fires," the Odawa, Chippewa, and Potawatomi. You have helped to take their fear of the Americans away. This is a great gift."

"All this from a dream?" asked Nick.

Chris shook his head and whispered to Nick. "I dreamed about race cars last night. I wonder if that means anything?"

The Chief stood before the boys and placed the turtle warrior back in Nicholas's hands.

"Meggie," whispered Nick, "if this rock means so much to the old Chief and your people, do you think they would like to keep it? It's just a rock. I have lots of them at home."

Meggie quickly spoke to the Chief whose eyes grew wide and sparkled. "I believe, Little Fawn, the Chief would like that very much," said Meggie.

Looking at the rock for one last time, Nick handed the turtle warrior to the Chief.

A man brought a beaded piece of leather to the Chief, who wrapped the turtle warrior rock in it carefully.

Chris leaned toward Nicholas and whispered, "You're a good kid!" Nick smiled and watched the Odawas as they gathered around their Chief and followed him out of the lodge. In his hands he carefully cradled the turtle stone.

Meggie watched as the last Odawa left the lodge. "You have given a very fine gift, Little Fawn. This is a special day for my people. This gift you have given is worth more than all of my trade goods. You have made them very happy."

"Meggie, I thought your people listened to the Black Robe Jesuits. They don't believe in dreams. Why do the Odawas think my dream and the turtle warrior rock are so special?"

"Yeah, anyone can have a dream," said Chris. "It doesn't make it come true, does it?"

"*Oui*, it is true the Black Robes visit L'Arbre Croche. But you must understand, my people are close to all things nature can provide. The sky, if it is clear, allows them to fish in the lake. The lake, if it is calm, allows them to travel to hunting grounds. And the rain, if it falls too hard, destroys the corn, squash, and beans. All things that happen in nature are important to the Odawa.

"That is why, when Great Mother Earth makes a rock in the form of a man or animal, it is special to the Odawa. And when a stranger who sleeps in their lodge dreams a good dream, this is a sign of good luck."

"Wow, I'm glad I didn't dream of monsters or anything like that," added Nick.

"Meggie, all this is great and everything, but we don't need to dream about monsters," said Chris. "What about McDougal and Grey Eyes? I am starting to get worried. What if they catch up with us here?"

"We have nothing to fear. The Odawa will help us now. But you are right. We must prepare to leave." Meggie spoke to LeClaire, who left the lodge, following the path to the lake.

"LeClaire goes to the canoe," said Meggie, "to gather our goods and prepare to depart."

Nick and Chris looked around the lodge, making sure they had all their clothes. Nick removed his warm blanket shirt and put on his own shirt.

"Man, I can't wait to get home, take a shower, and change my clothes. How about you, Chris?"

Chris looked at Nicholas and scrunched his eyes. "You know, Nick sometimes you can be a real geek."

Meggie packed her small bundles, leaving several strings of beads and a mirror near the fire as a gift to the women of the lodge.

Chris began to search the lodge, realizing for the first time, that he was missing something. "Hey, has anyone seen my red canteen?" He lifted the fur robes from the mats and looked in all the baskets.

"Chris, don't worry. It's probably with the paddles," said Nick.

"Yeah, but I'd hate to lose it. It was a gift from Mom and Dad at Christmas."

Nick remembered when Chris had un-wrapped the canteen at Christmastime, and how surprised he had been that they had remembered he wanted one for his walks on the dunes and in the woods.

Nick wondered if he and Chris would ever have another Christmas at home, sitting around the family Christmas tree, singing Christmas carols and munching on cookies. I bet the Odawas don't celebrate Christmas like that, Nick thought to himself.

Just then a loud blast was heard from outside. Nick, startled from his daydream, quickly looked at Meggie and Chris. "I bet it's McDougal!" he shouted. "Meggie, what do we do?"

"Stay in the lodge. I will return." Meggie darted out the blanketed door and scooted along behind the lodges to the lake harbor.

There, approaching shore, was the small canoe carrying McDougal and Grey Eyes. McDougal, standing in the front of the canoe, held his gun high and shot off another blast. His mouth opened wide, as he shouted for the Odawas to give him aid. Meggie could see Grey Eyes wading in the water, guiding the canoe to shore.

The people gathered along the shore, not returning the calls or making any shouts of welcome. McDougal again called to the Odawas along the shore, ordering them to help. The Odawa men slowly waded out into the water toward the canoe.

As they approached, the canoe suddenly caught fast on something in the water, jerking it forward. McDougal lunged backward onto the floor of the canoe, with his feet sticking straight up in the air.

"Ye renegade dog! Ye did that on purpose!" McDougal howled from the bottom of the canoe.

The Odawas along the shore laughed at the funny sight. Meggie, who was watching from behind the lodge, wished McDougal had fallen into the water. Maybe a bath would have washed away his meanness.

LeClaire joined Meggie and watched the two Devils come ashore. They knew the time was near for them to make their escape. But when they returned to the lodge to summon Chris and Nick, Meggie and LeClaire found no trace of the two boys.

LeClaire ran outside, thinking they might have followed Meggie to the shore. Inside, Meggie wondered where the boys might have gone.

All of a sudden, Meggie heard an a-a-a-choo! It came from beneath a pile of fur robes lying in the corner of the lodge. Lifting the corner of a robe, she found Nick and Chris, hiding.

"Nice going, Nick. If that was McDougal, we'd be done for."

"I'm sorry," said Nick, "but the fur got in my nose."

Meggie smiled at the boys. "Hiding from the enemy is a wise thing to do," she said.

"It was Nick's idea," said Chris. "I should have known it wouldn't work."

"Is McDougal here?"

"*Oui*, the Devils have arrived."

LeClaire entered the lodge. Spying the boys, he gave them both a fierce look."This is no time for games. Where did you go?"

Meggie explained to LeClaire that the boys were only hiding. LeClaire didn't think that was such a good idea and flashed the boys another angry look.

"Make ready!" demanded LeClaire. "The Chief wants us to wait. He sends someone to get us when it is time."

Meggie, Chris, and Nick sat quietly beside the fire while LeClaire kept guard at the blanketed door.

Chapter 11
The Traders' Feast

On the beach, the Odawas gathered to hear all McDougal had to say.

"*Bonjour, bonjour*," he called to them as he waded ashore. "Ye come to give good trade? I come to seek help."

The old Chief stood on the shore and spoke to his people in Algonquin, a language that McDougal could not understand but Grey Eyes knew well.

The Chief, seeing the scar on Grey Eyes' face, knew this was the bad renegade Métis. He knew he would have to be careful what he said.

The Chief called to his people to bring their furs out of their lodges to make big trade with the great McDougal. The old Chief also called to the women to prepare a feast to feed the hungry men. This, he thought, would keep them busy and give Meggie, LeClaire, and the boys time to escape.

"I don't want ye many furs now! I come for help," snapped McDougal. The men came out of their lodges with their arms filled with fur pelts.

"Did a vessel come here with two boys, on its way to the island of the turtle?" demanded McDougal.

Receiving no reply, McDougal snapped, "Grey Eyes, tell these people what I said!"

Grey Eyes glared at McDougal's order, but translated what was said into Algonquin.

The men replied, "*Kaw* (no)!"

This made McDougal angry. "They can't be tellin' the truth. This is the only harbor they could make to before the island," shouted McDougal.

"Grey, tell 'em if they ain't tellin' the truth, I'll have the Americans pay 'em a visit." McDougal's lips curled back in a snarl, showing the holes from his missing teeth.

Grey Eyes spoke to the Odawas, telling them what McDougal had said. When the Odawa men heard the threat, they laughed and walked away, leaving McDougal and Grey Eyes on the beach.

"What ye say to 'em, ye renegade? What ye tell 'em to make 'em leave?" McDougal shouted at Grey Eyes.

Angered by the way McDougal spoke to him, Grey Eyes shrugged his shoulders and followed the men of the village toward their lodges, leaving McDougal on the beach alone.

In the village, in front of the Chief's lodge, lay great piles of furs—soft brown muskrat, thick black beaver, bearskins and piles of deerskins, all from the men's winter hunt.

"No, Grey, tell 'em, we don't want trade. Tell 'em we want information," demanded McDougal, as he chased into the village after Grey Eyes.

Grey Eyes began pleading with the Odawas, who pretended not to understand what the two Devils wanted. Soon the women came from their lodges with bowls of food left from the feast the night before. A large Indian man put his hands on McDougal's shoulders and pushed him to the ground to sit and eat. Another grabbed Grey Eyes and tried to push him down beside McDougal. Grey Eyes pulled back with a fierce look in his eyes.

"Ol' Grey, ye might as well give up an come eat. These savages might even have a drop of rum for us. What ye think?" said McDougal.

Grey Eyes, suspicious of what was going on, sat silently beside McDougal and watched the women as they walked in and out of their lodges, bringing more food.

"D'is no good, not right," whispered Grey Eyes to McDougal.

"Come on, these people have finally come to their senses. They're tryin' to please me. Eat!" ordered McDougal. "We'll talk afterward."

Grey Eyes sat beside McDougal, who ate greedily from the bowls of food.

LeClaire, watching from behind the lodge blanket, could see the two Devils as they ate and drank. "Meggie," said LeClaire, "the Chief has ordered our canoe to be taken to a cove not far from here. When it's ready, we will be led to the cove.

"The starving dogs, Grey Eyes and McDougal, make themselves fat on our joke," he said and smiled.

Soon someone appeared at the blanketed door. It was Waugoshance (Little Fox). LeClaire let the girl enter.

Chris, recognizing the girl, called to Nick. "Hey Nick, your girlfriend's here."

The girl smiled at Nick and motioned for him and the others to follow her to their canoe. Picking up their bundles, they slipped out of the lodge to a path behind the village without anyone seeing them. The path was smooth and clear and appeared to have been there for a long time. It led through an opening in the forest beside the harbor.

Little Fox ran ahead and everyone followed. The path turned along the shoreline. There, in an area covered over with low-hanging branches, sat the canoe.

Two men carried Meggie to the canoe while another held it steady in the water. The men returned to shore, and one carried Nicholas to the canoe. Nick waved good-bye to Waugoshance, who waved back.

As Nick got settled, he could see the Indian girl Wau-wass kona (Flower) standing behind Chris. She carried Chris's red canteen in her hands.

"Chris, look!" called Nick.

Chris turned. The girl held the canteen, full of fresh water, out to him. "Wow, my canteen, thanks!" Chris grabbed it and smiled at the girl, "This is great! It's full and everything. I've got to go, OK? Bye!" The girl smiled back at Chris.

The men who stood on shore allowed Chris to wade out to the canoe so he wouldn't be embarrassed. Before he got to the canoe, however, he spied a pretty, white water lily growing in the water. Bending down, he reached into the water and plucked the flower from its roots. Quickly wading back to shore, he placed it in the girl's hand and smiled. Then he splashed back to the canoe and crawled in.

On the beach, Little Fox and Flower stood together, waving and calling "*bo-jo, bo-jo*" as the canoe left the cove. "Oh, Chris, I'm gonna tell Mom you've got a girlfriend," teased Nick.

Crawling into the back of the canoe, LeClaire remarked to Chris, "A little flower for a little flower, *très bien*! You must be part French, my friend. Frenchmen have an eye for beauty." With that, the canoe cleared the cove, heading for the mouth of the inlet.

"LeClaire," asked Chris, "do you think we can make the island before McDougal catches us?"

"*Oui*, we will be in the big lake soon, and the Chief has ordered Le Diable's canoe set adrift. When they discover they have been tricked, it will take them time to get their canoe."

"I like that," said Chris.

"*Oui*, so do I," said Meggie.

The crew paddled into the mouth of the inlet and started toward Lake Michigan. The water was calm now that the storm had passed.

"How far to the island, LeClaire?" asked Nick.

"About five pipes. Not far. There you will be safe."

"We will need to talk to the Black Robe as soon as we get there," said Nick. "Right, Meggie?"

"*Oui*, as soon as we can."

Meanwhile, back at the village, McDougal and Grey Eyes were just finishing their feast when the old Chief brought out something very special to show his guests. It was a piece of beaded leather, and wrapped inside was the turtle warrior rock.

The old Chief opened the leather wrap that held the stone turtle. Leaning close, he showed it to McDougal and Grey Eyes.

Grey Eyes, spying the rock, flew into a rage. "They play a trick," shouted Grey Eyes.

"Sit yerself down, ye upset the ol' Chief here," said McDougal. The Chief, moving back, realized something was wrong. Quickly, he wrapped the turtle warrior back up in its beaded leather covering and disappeared into his lodge.

"McDougal, that is the boy's rock! The rock by the water barrel. They helped him escape!"

McDougal thought for a moment. Looking into the faces of the people who surrounded him, he could see something was wrong.

Flying to his feet, McDougal grabbed his rifle and ran to the shore with Grey Eyes following. "See, in the water," pointed Grey Eyes. "At the mouth of the lake there is a canoe." Grey Eyes waded out into the water and stared at the horizon. In a panic he realized, "Our canoe is gone!"

"The canoe, the canoe, it is gone," Grey Eyes shouted again.

"Blast ye! Where's my canoe?" McDougal screeched at the men along the beach.

"There!" Grey Eyes pointed. And sure enough, some way down the beach, the little canoe had washed ashore. Grey Eyes waded into the water while McDougal ran along the sand. Soon catching hold of their canoe, they lifted it carefully off the sand and directed it to the mouth of the harbor.

Once the canoe was away from shore, they crawled in. McDougal shouted orders to Grey Eyes. Looking back at the shore where the villagers stood, he shook his fist. "I'll be havin' the Americans after ye now."

Quickly loading his gun, he stood in the front of the canoe and fired! But in the rush he had put too much gun powder in the barrel. The gun bolted back, throwing McDougal to the floor of the canoe.

As the villagers left the beach, they covered the ears of their children so they would not hear McDougal's screams and curses carrying across the water.

Meggie and LeClaire heard the blast from McDougal's rifle. They knew they had been found out. "The Devil is on our trail," called LeClaire, while steering the canoe into deeper water. Meggie picked up the pace with her paddle, and the boys joined in.

"Put on the paddle-power," called Chris. The boys quickly dug the water with their red paddles, moving the canoe swiftly forward. Grey Eyes and McDougal, however, were catching up. Their canoe, now at the mouth of the inlet, bounced up and down on the waves.

Chapter 12
The Great Canoe Race

"Meggie," called Nick, "you forgot the offering for a safe journey."

"*Oui*, it will have to wait, for the Devil is close behind." said Meggie.

"If the Devil is close behind," said Chris, "I think it would be a good time to make an offering."

LeClaire reached his paddle out from the canoe and brought the canoe to a steady position. "The boy is right!" LeClaire handed his tobacco bag forward to Meggie.

Meggie, quickly standing, sang her offering song and scattered the tobacco into the water.

"Look!" screeched McDougal. "The Mètis she's stopped to make an offering. Now's our chance! Paddle faster, Grey."

Grey Eyes, hungry for money, growled low and thought about the many coins that would come from the sale of the two boys. His paddle flashed in the water as he gained speed to overtake the larger canoe.

Meggie, still standing in the canoe, could now see the reflection of Joseph's cross as it flashed upon the water. "The Devil is upon us," she called and quickly sat to resume paddling.

"Steady her, steady the blasted canoe," bellowed McDougal to Grey Eyes. "If ye steady her, I can load me gun. I got a clear shot to sink the birchbark! Then we grab the boys!"

McDougal pulled his rifle forward from the canoe. Opening his powder horn, he carefully poured the grainy black gun powder down the throat of the rifle. With each bounce of a wave, McDougal spilled some of the precious powder into the canoe.

"That should do 'er," he said, slamming the cork back into the powder horn. Taking out his ramrod from the side of the barrel, he slapped the powder tight. Placing a patch and lead ball into the gun, he slammed it all again with the rod. McDougal was ready!

"Aarrr," he growled to Grey Eyes. "They'll be money in our pockets by the end of this day. Right ol' Grey?"

"Be no money if the canoe gets to the Ile de Michilimackinac before us," called Grey Eyes.

McDougal looked up and could see Meggie's canoe rounding a point of land ahead of them.

And there, directly ahead, was the misty outline of Mackinac Island.

"Look," called Chris, "I think I can see the island." LeClaire and Meggie dug their paddles into the water even harder. The boys had trouble keeping up. The pace of the paddles beat one stroke a second, sixty strokes a minute.

Oui, the boy is right. We are almost in safe waters, thought Meggie. Le Diable Rouge would dare not follow too close to the island, for it will be his end.

"Faster, faster," called Nick, watching as they left the Red Devil behind.

"Paddle, paddle now, you renegade. They're out of range," growled McDougal.

Grey Eyes grabbed a second paddle from the floor of the canoe and threw it forward, hitting McDougal across the shoulder.

"You paddle, too," demanded Grey Eyes.

McDougal, resting his rifle to his side, squatted to his knees and grabbed up the paddle, dipping it into the water, paddling faster and faster. With each stroke of the paddle, the canoe rode high on the waves and then slammed back down, spraying the inside of the canoe with water.

McDougal could only think about getting closer—closer to his prize.

Meggie, Nicholas, Christopher, and LeClaire paddled so fast in their canoe that they looked like a giant water bug with red feet scurrying across the top of the water.

Nicholas's arms and hands were tired. He wanted to rest.

"Keep paddling," called LeClaire. "We are almost there." Sprays of water splashed into the canoe, as the paddles dug the waves.

Grey Eye's little canoe was catching up to them. The two Devils cut the waves with their paddles as they bounced high into the air. Water splashed in all directions, soaking them to the skin.

"The bath'll be worth the reward, ol' Grey," called McDougal. "Now steady the canoe, so I can get a shot off."

Grey Eyes reached out his paddle, trying to steady the canoe on the waves. McDougal filled the pan with gunpowder, so it would take under the strike of the flint. Standing tall in the canoe, McDougal took a deep breath and snapped the trigger. Nothing happened.

"What in blue blazes!" he snarled.

A grey-blue puff of smoke filled the air around McDougal's head. Grey Eyes wasn't sure if the smoke was from McDougal's gun or from his anger.

"Me powder's wet!" he howled.

Just then a large wave slapped the side of the small canoe, sending it sidewise across the water. McDougal lost his balance and sprawled over the front end of the canoe, nearly falling into the lake. His feet, caught on the canoe's edge, held McDougal as he hung over the front and bounced up and down in the waves.

"Me gun, me gun—it's fallen inta the water!" McDougal hung over the end and peered deep into the lake.

"The water, she's got me gun! Ye blasted renegade, what'll I do?"

Grey Eyes glared at McDougal and barked, "Paddle!"

Meggie and LeClaire, who had no idea how close they almost came to being shot at, paddled swiftly toward the island, which they could now plainly see. There, above the harbor, stood the white stone fort.

"Wow, Chris, we're almost there!" shouted Nick.

"Keep paddling, Nick," yelled Chris.

McDougal and Grey Eyes increased their speed as they paddled together, knowing the only way to capture their prize now would be to overtake the canoe.

LeClaire knew if the two Devils really tried, they could catch up. His muscles ached as he paddled across the straits, pointing the canoe straight into the island's harbor. If only the soldiers at the fort would see them, he thought, then they would have a chance.

McDougal was fast approaching. Over the splashing of the waves the boys could hear him yelling orders to Grey Eyes.

Out of the corner of his eye, LeClaire could now see the flash of light reflecting off Joseph's cross, which hung around the throat of the Devil.

"They're right behind us!" yelled Nick.

Meggie turned, looking into the red eyes of the Devil, McDougal. Their canoes now rode the waves side by side.

LeClaire stuck out his long paddle, bumping and pushing the small canoe away from them.

Grey Eyes splashed out with his paddle, slamming it hard against LeClaire's

Meggie picked up the small bundles lying at her feet and threw them at McDougal. McDougal laughed, the black gap between his front teeth showing wide.

"Ye throwing me food?" McDougal jeered. "No thanks. I had me feast at Crooked Tree."

Meggie could see Joseph's pendant around McDougal's throat. I must be brave, I must be brave, she thought to herself.

Just then, a loud blast came from the island fort. It was the fort's cannon. A puff of smoke, hanging in the air, could plainly be seen at the top of the hill where the fort stood.

"It's the soldiers," called Meggie. "They have seen us."

LeClaire directed the canoe in a zigzag motion, trying to keep McDougal from catching hold of them.

"Leave us alone, you jerks," Nick called out in fear.

Grey Eyes, steering his canoe directly into the path of LeClaire, slammed hard against the canoe's side.

The boys hung on for their lives as Grey Eyes and LeClaire slapped paddles, back and forth, at each other. Grey Eyes, taking careful aim, smashed his paddle down on top of LeClaire's hand.

LeClaire, losing his grip, watched as his paddle spun through the air, then fell into the water.

"We got ye now," snarled McDougal.

Meggie slapped at him with her paddle, trying to keep him from grabbing the canoe.

Grey Eyes stood and seized LeClaire's arm, pulling the canoes closer together.

"Nick," yelled Chris, "get my canteen."

Nick reached behind, grabbed the canteen, and tossed it to him. Chris, standing carefully, started swinging the canteen by its strap above his head. Round and round it went, swinging faster and faster. Then Chris let go of the strap, sending the canteen sailing through the air and whacking Grey Eyes right in the stomach.

Losing his balance, Grey Eyes tumbled out of the canoe into the water, almost pulling McDougal with him.

"Grey, Grey," screamed McDougal. "Where'd ye go? Ye know ye can't swim!"

"Good going, Chris!" hollered Nick.

Angered by the fight, LeClaire pulled out his long blue steel knife and slashed McDougal's canoe, making a long, jagged rip along it's side.

Meggie, seeing her chance to help, pushed the Devil's canoe away with her paddle and set them adrift.

McDougal, who was busy fishing Grey Eyes out of the water, didn't notice that the canoe had started taking on water. Back in the canoe, Grey Eyes coughed and spit up water. Once he had caught his breath, he noticed the hole in the canoe.

LeClaire grabbed Nick's paddle from the floor and began to paddle away from the two Devils.

"Hey, hey, hold up! Ye can't go, ye can't go. We can't swim," pleaded McDougal. Meggie and Chris picked up their paddles and joined LeClaire.

Grey Eyes and McDougal began bailing the water out of their canoe with their hands.

Just then a gun blast was heard from over the water. There, straight in front of them, were two canoes filled with men from the island.

"Blast it!" howled McDougal. "We're done for!" and he sat in the floor of the sinking canoe with water almost up to his waist. Grey Eyes, with his long wet hair hanging limply around his face, threw back his head and howled like a wolf.

Chris and Nick laughed. "He sounds like a wet puppy," said Nick.

Meggie, LeClaire, and Christopher paddled forward, meeting the approaching canoes.

Shouts of *"Bonjour,* Meggie, *Bonjour,* LeClaire,"* filled the air. In the two canoes, there was a strange and wonderful array of men. Some were soldiers in red jackets like the one worn by the Chief at Crooked Tree. Others were wrapped in blankets with feathers blowing in their hair. And still others, the Frenchmen, wore knitted hats and colorful shirts.

From one of the canoes, a soldier threw a rope to LeClaire to secure his canoe. The soldiers were going to tow LeClaire's crew into the harbor. The other boat approached the canoe of the two Devils.

"We did it!" yelled Chris. "We made it!"

Nick, tired from the ordeal, laid his head down along the side of the canoe and was very quiet.

LeClaire took Meggie's long paddle and gently guided the canoe along as it was pulled by the soldiers and voyageurs.

Stretching his legs, Chris sat flat on the canoe bottom. His knees ached and his hands were red and blistered. He turned to LeClaire and showed him his hands. "I guess I didn't use enough bear grease!"

"*Oui*," said LeClaire as he reached out and patted Chris on the back with the paddle. "You did a fine job today. I am proud you are in my canoe."

Meggie turned and smiled a tired grin at Christopher. She noticed Nicholas, Little Fawn, had fallen asleep.

Chapter 13

The Island

The waves bumped against the canoe, gently lifting it up and down as it was towed toward the island's harbor. Following close behind were McDougal and Grey Eyes, being towed in their canoe as it slowly filled with water. Laughter rang out from the soldiers as they watched Grey Eyes and McDougal frantically bail their canoe with their bare hands.

"All right, ye rascals, ye gat us. Now git us outta this leaky canoe!" howled McDougal. The soldiers and voyageurs watched and waved at them, mocking McDougal's anger.

Chris looked back in fear when he heard McDougal's loud voice, a voice he knew he would never forget.

"Hey, Nick, look! Wake up. You gotta see this!" said Chris as he shook Nicholas awake.

Looking back, Nick could see McDougal in his sinking vessel, shouting and waving his fists in the air at the soldiers.

"The Captain, he teaches our enemies a lesson, no?" said LeClaire, who had a big grin of satisfaction on his face.

"He teaches a good lesson, yes!" responded Christopher.

McDougal's and Grey Eyes' canoe soon filled up completely with water and began to sink. The two Devils, abandoning their craft, plunged into the cold water of the lake. Splashing around, they flailed their arms in all directions as they tried to keep afloat. The towline pulling their canoe was cut, and the body of the small birchbark sank below the surface of the water. Voyageurs and soldiers, with paddles in hand, reached out toward the two men to help them.

McDougal and Grey Eyes, stretching out their arms, desperately tried to grasp onto the paddles to save themselves from sinking.

"Sorry, Mister McDougal, Mister Grey, sir—" called the Captain of the soldiers. "There will be no room in this vessel for the likes of you two. Right men?" The soldiers, catching onto the joke, all responded with a roar of laughter as they pulled their paddles into the canoe.

"Mister McDougal, sir, you and your friend will have to be towed to the dock. I hope you like ta swim!"

"Cast them a line, boys," the Captain ordered. And the long tow rope that had pulled the sinking birchbark was thrown to McDougal and Grey Eyes.

The two Devils, half drowned and exhausted, grabbed the rope and hung on for their lives.

The order was given, "Make for the wharf, boys." The soldiers and voyageurs dug their red paddles deep into the swelling waves and headed toward the island's dock.

McDougal and Grey Eyes held tight to the rope as the waves scooped them up and dipped them under. "If ye don't get me inta ye boat," bellowed McDougal to the Captain. "I'll—I'll—" A wave silenced McDougal, dipping him under the water. When he popped back up, he coughed and spit, clinging silently to the rope.

Grey Eyes, knowing his defeat, quietly held onto the towline and tried to keep his head above the water.

The soldiers and voyageurs paddled together, pulling their cargo closer to the island. Soon one of the voyageurs began calling out the words to a new song he had just made up. It was about two great fish that got caught—one as red as the Devil and the other with a scar on its face.

The song carried across the water to LeClaire, who joined in the fun, singing loudly. Meggie smiled to herself and began clapping her hands to the rhythm.

"That's a good song, LeClaire!" called Nick.

"*Oui*, Little Fawn, it is a fine song. I will sing it often when I remember our adventures."

The canoes came nearer and nearer the island. Chris and Nick could see people gathering along the shore. Some were shooting their guns while others waved and threw their hats high into the air. The beach, as far as the eyes could see, was covered with people, tents, and small Indian lodges.

"Wow, Nick! Check this out! It looks like a campground in the summer. There must be a thousand people camped on the beach!"

"*Oui*. It is rendezvous time. As in your dream, Little Fawn," said Meggie, "the inhabitants return from their wintering post with their furs to take them to the warehouses. The voyageurs, with their families, wait for the next brigade to go out. And many Indian tribes, they come to trade their furs and receive payment for their land. It is a time of celebration!"

The towline to LeClaire's canoe soon tugged and slapped the water as it dropped. The soldiers who had been towing them turned and waved. They were all safe at Ile de Michilimackinac. Meggie and LeClaire picked up their paddles and paddled the birchbark into the harbor and up to the wharf, which loomed high above the waterline.

The soldiers and voyageurs in the first canoe had already secured their canoe to the wharf and were waiting to help LeClaire. They tied LeClaire's canoe to the dock and lifted Meggie and the boys up onto the wharf.

A crowd which had gathered met them with calls of "greetings" and "hurrah!" Voyageurs, dressed in a wild array of colors, greeted LeClaire, slapping him on the back and calling, "*Bonjour, mon ami!*" Meggie was greeted with hugs and handfuls of wild flowers, while little children danced around her in their excitement.

"I guess Meggie and LeClaire have lots of friends on the island," agreed the boys.

The canoe towing McDougal and Grey Eyes now approached the wharf. The Captain, throwing a line onto the dock, secured it. Once it was in place he shouted the order, "Bring the fish in, boys!"

Pulling in the towline, the men hauled McDougal and Grey Eyes from the water into the canoe. Dripping wet and exhausted, they stood wobbly-legged. Some soldiers on the dock pulled the two Devils up out of the canoe. McDougal and Grey Eyes dropped to their knees, trying to recover from their ordeal.

More soldiers came down from the hill fort, greeting the Captain and pulling the two wet Devils to their feet. Then they escorted them through the crowd toward the stone fort.

"Monsieur LeClaire, Madame La Framboise," said the Captain, "as soon as you rest yourselves, I'll need to speak to you at the fort."

"*Oui*, Captain," said LeClaire. "The Red Devil has finally been caught, no?"

"Thanks be to your help. The trade agent here at Mackinac will be glad to see those two behind bars. They've been cheating and stealing from legal traders for years. These two will do anything for coins in their pocket."

"That's for sure!" added Chris.

The shout of "hurrah" rang through the crowd and high into the air as the Captain and his men left the wharf.

A brightly dressed voyageur with long hair and a beard picked Nicholas up high onto his shoulder and danced with him through the crowd. Everyone laughed and shouted in a mixture of different languages. The meaning was clear, however. The Indians, the French, the English, and the Métis were all happy that McDougal and Grey Eyes were finally caught.

Nick, sitting on the shoulder of the voyageur, could see beyond the crowd. There in the distance, heading up the hill after the soldiers, was LeClaire, running to catch up to the Captain. Spying LeClaire, the Captain brought his men to a halt.

Nick could see LeClaire and the Captain talking. They both walked slowly over to McDougal, who tried to pull away. The soldiers held him tight and LeClaire pulled something from around his neck. It must be Meggie's pendant, thought Nick.

LeClaire bid the soldiers good-bye and soon returned, running down the hill. The soldiers pushed McDougal back into line and continued their march. They soon entered the fort through a narrow gate and disappeared from sight.

On the beach the voyageur set Nicholas down on the ground, where people began to crowd around him. Everyone wanted to hear the tale that lead to the capture of the Le Diable Rouge.

"Chris," said Nick, "this looks like a great big circus with everyone in costumes!"

British soldiers dressed in their bright red coats and tall hats mingled among Indians wrapped in colorful blankets. Voyageurs dressed in bright shirts and sashes mixed with ladies in long skirts and bonnets. And there, standing in the middle of the crowd, Nicholas spied LeClaire.

"Chris, look. There's LeClaire. Get Meggie. I think he's got something for her."

Chris, looking around in all the confusion, searched the crowd until he found Meggie. She was telling her tale to a group of traders who stood wide-eyed, listening to the adventure.

"Meggie!" called Chris, "I think LeClaire is looking for you!"

When Meggie turned to face Christopher, LeClaire walked up from behind Chris, holding his hand out to her, the pendant dangling from its black ribbon.

"Madame, your pendant," he said bowing low from the waist.

Meggie, delighted to see her treasure, grasped it from LeClaire's hand and quickly tied it around her neck.

"*Merci, mon ami* (Thank you, my friend)," she said with tears in her eyes.

"*Merci, merci*, to you all," she said, holding her arms out to the boys and giving them a big hug. A shout of "hurrah" rang out again from the crowd. Nick was glad Meggie had gotten her pendant back, but deep inside he wished LeClaire would have brought him his turtle warrior rock, too.

Chris, standing beside Nicholas, looked at him and asked, "Do you wish you had your turtle warrior?"

"How did you know what I was thinking?" returned a suprised Nicholas.

"Hey, we're brothers, aren't we? You know, I bet some day you'll see that old turtle rock again. It'll pop up some place, just like when you found it at the top of the dune."

"Do you really think so?"

"Sure. You've got a knack for finding special rocks." Nick smiled and was glad he and his brother were together and that they had shared this great adventure.

Soon an old bearded man on the beach wearing a bright, red shirt and sash began to play a fiddle. Many people in the crowd made a wide, open circle and began clapping their hands while others danced.

"This is great," said Chris. "Look at everyone having fun!"

"Boys!" called Meggie loudly to get their attention. "Are you hungry?"

"I'm starved," shouted Chris in the excitement.

"Follow me. We eat!" Meggie motioned for the boys to follow her through the crowd. They soon came to a small beach lodge where a big, black kettle of soup was simmering over a fire.

"Hey, I smell Mackinac," shouted Chris. "It smells like fish and furs, bubbling soup and sunshine!" Everyone could tell Christopher was happy to be at Mackinac.

"You forgot something," added LeClaire jokingly.

"What's that?" asked Chris.

"The smell of a young American voyageur! Phew!"

"Hey, that's not funny, LeClaire. I don't smell!" insisted Chris.

"Oh yeah!" added Nick, laughing and jumping around in the sand, holding his nose. Chris ran after Nick down the beach, tackling him and pulling him to the sand, laughing.

An Indian woman who was a friend of Meggie's brought wooden bowls from her lodge and served up the steaming soup from the kettle. Chris and Nick, dusting sand out of their hair, sat down by the fire to eat. The soup felt good in their empty stomachs after a day of such hard work and high drama.

"Meggie?" said Nick. "You said you would take us to see the Black Robe when we got to the island. Remember?"

"*Oui*, Little Fawn, I remember." Meggie stood and spoke in Algonquin to the Indian woman, asking her about the Black Robe.

"Is this lady Odawa?" whispered Nick to LeClaire.

"*Oui*. She is from Gabagouache," he answered.

"Chris, this lady is from Gabagouache— Grand Haven. She could be our neighbor!"

The lady spoke quietly with Meggie, pointing up the beach along the shore. Turning to the boys, Meggie had a worried look on her face.

"Little Fawn," she said, "my friend tells me the Black Robe has not visited the island in many moons. He lives across the water at the mission and no one has seen him for a long time."

"Meggie, can't you take us there? We can look for him," insisted Nick.

"*Oui*. LeClaire can take you to the mission, but sometimes the Black Robe goes deep into the *pays du haut* (north country). There he teaches his ways to the many different tribes. He may not return to the mission for a full season."

Nick hung his head low. "Chris," he said, "what are we going to do? We've got to get back home!"

"I don't know, little brother, but everything will work out. Meggie and LeClaire will see to that. Don't be scared now. We're almost home!" said Chris.

"I will send a messenger to the mission," said Meggie. "There is a chance we may reach him. Do not be afraid, Little Fawn. Be brave!"

Nick had a hard time finishing his soup as he tried to fight back his tears. What if we never get back home, he thought to himself.

Chris put his arm around Nick as they both sat watching the crowd of people on the beach. The Indian woman offered the boys more soup, but they had lost their appetite.

When he finished eating, LeClaire stood tall and rubbed his belly. "I go now to find a canoe man to deliver the message to the Black Robe. Come with me. I will show you the village on this island."

"I don't feel much like sightseeing, LeClaire. Thanks anyway," said Nick.

Chris quickly jumped to his feet and pulled on Nicholas' arm. "Come on, get up, Nick. This sounds like fun!"

"Little Fawn, it is good you go. If the Black Robe comes and returns you to your time, you may never see the village again at rendezvous." Meggie looked at Nicholas and wiped the tears from his face.

"She's right, Nick," said Chris. "This might be your last chance."

Nick slowly got to his feet and dusted the sand from his pants. "I guess you're right," he said and followed LeClaire and Chris through the crowd toward the village.

The village of Mackinac, which was not very big, stretched out along the beach. Most of its buildings were small and looked like huts. There were a few houses that were made of rough-cut logs and looked like Meggie's cabin.

"Wow! This is really different," said Chris. Where are all the big buildings and houses and hotels like we see on the island in our time? I thought those were supposed to be old. The only thing that looks the same is the fort and the water."

"Yeah, but Chris, the water isn't the same either. There's no bridge crossing the straits!" said Nick.

"A bridge crossing water? Surely you joke with LeClaire?" Their giant friend was amazed by the idea of a bridge crossing the vast water of the straits.

"It's not a joke, LeClaire. In our time, there is this great big bridge and people cross over it to get to St. Ignace on the other side of the strait," said Nick.

"You still have to ride a boat to get to this island, though." added Chris.

"*Sainte Ignatius? Oui!* That is where the mission of the Black Robe is. I believe when Americans come to our island many wonderful things will take place!"

Chris and Nick smiled, thinking about all the many changes that would take place on the island in the next two hundred years. The Americans would come, but the British would try and steal the island back again. Then all the soldiers would leave, and eventually the fort would be made into a museum. The island would become a state park, bringing thousands of visitors from all over the world. Time sure can change things, the boys thought.

"Hey, Chris, look!" called Nick as he pointed to a small hut that resembled a lemonade stand. Several men stood around the outside of the hut, smoking their pipes and looking at all sorts of trinkets.

"That is a trader's booth," said LeClaire. "Some of the traders put them up when they visit the island in the summer."

"It looks like the first tourist stand to me!" said Chris laughing.

The boys followed LeClaire up a short dirt road that led to a second row of small bark and log-covered houses. He stopped in front of one that was being built. LeClaire called to a man who stood in the side yard, sawing wood."

"*Bonjour*, Edward!" called LeClaire.

The man looked up from his work and smiled. Laying his saw aside, he joined LeClaire, shaking hands.

"This, my friends," LeClaire said to the boys, "is Monsieur Biddle. Maybe he will help us with our task. What do you think?"

The man, older than LeClaire, had a smile on his face that made Nicholas feel like smiling. I sure hope he can help us, thought Nick.

LeClaire and Biddle walked off together as Biddle showed him the work being done on the new cabin. Nicholas watched as the two men talked. Soon they shook hands again. A deal had been made, thought Nick.

When LeClaire returned he announced, "Monsieur Biddle will arrange for the message to be delivered to the mission tomorrow. The Black Robe will be found and brought to the island, no matter how many moons it takes."

"I hope it's not too many moons," said Nick.

"See Nick, everything will work out," Chris said, patting his brother on the back.

"LeClaire?" asked Nick. "When did you say the Americans were coming to the island? Maybe they will be able to help us."

"I am told the Americans were expected to take the fort in the strawberry moon."

"The strawberry moon? When's that?" asked Nick.

"I bet I know," said Chris. "I bet it's when the strawberries are ready to pick. Right?"

"*Oui*, the strawberries."

"That's now!" said Chris. "Nick, don't you remember Mom asking us if we wanted to help her pick strawberries next week for the freezer?"

Nick thought for a moment, strawberries for the freezer. Wow! That seemed like a long time ago.

"So the strawberry moon must mean June," added Chris. "The Americans are due here this month."

"Monsieur Biddle, however, has told me the British officers have made a deal with the Americans. The Americans have agreed to come to the island after rendezvous— after everyone has left for their wintering place and before the ice blocks the straits. That way, there will be no trouble."

"Boy, I sure would have liked to see one of those big ships with all their sails bringing American soldiers to the island. That would have been neat! Too bad we'll be home by then, right Nick?" asked Chris.

"Yeah, you're right. That would have been neat, but I'd rather be home reading about it," responded Nick.

Nick and Chris spent the rest of the afternoon walking around the small village, looking into traders' booths and waiting for LeClaire as he told his many friends the tale of the two Devils. Finally the three made their way back through the village to the beach lodge of Meggie's friend.

Chapter 14
Home

No sooner had they returned to the lodge than gunshots were heard. The people began gathering on the beach once more, and shouts of "welcome" sounded through the crowd.

"A canoe approaches," said Meggie to the boys. Several Indian women passing by the lodge called to Meggie's friend in Algonquin. A woman with an excited look on her face spoke to Meggie.

"It is a miracle!" called Meggie. "The Black Robe—he has come to the island."

"The Black Robe! Nick, did you hear that? The Black Robe has come!" shouted Chris.

Nick jumped up and danced around in his excitement. "Meggie, let's go see him!"

"It is best, Little Fawn," said LeClaire in a serious voice, "that we wait until the people escort the Black Robe to the chapel of Sainte Anne. There we may speak with him privately."

"LeClaire is right," added Meggie. "All the people are happy to see the Black Robe. It will be impossible to talk with him until he reaches the chapel."

"LeClaire," asked Nick, "do you think your friend Biddle sent someone to the mission already?"

"No, it is not possible, Little Fawn," said LeClaire. "The Black Robe has come because he knows you have need of him. As Madame told you, he is very special and knows many things."

"See, Nick, this guy will be able to help us. He already knows we need him," joined in Chris.

Nick watched as a crowd slowly made its way up the beach, moving toward the village. Nick couldn't see anyone who looked like someone special to him, but in the middle of the crowd walked the Black Robe.

The boys sat on the beach watching the little dogs and children play and throwing stones into the lake. Time seemed to pass very slowly.

Soon the sun will be setting thought Nick. We won't be able to get back home tonight if we wait much longer.

Meggie spoke softly to LeClaire, who was starting to doze by the fire. LeClaire awoke, stretched his arms, and yawned. Standing tall, he looked down at the boys.

"Why is it you wait? Do you not wish to see the Black Robe?" he joked. "It is time we go hear what the Black Robe has to tell you."

Meggie stood by the fire with a sad look on her face. "*Mon amis*, LeClaire and I will tell you good-bye now."

"The Black Robe, if he can help you, will not want to waste time for good-byes," agreed LeClaire.

Nick smiled up at LeClaire, who put out his big hand to shake with Nicholas. Shrugging his shoulders, Nicholas reached up, giving LeClaire a big hug. Meggie reached out to Christopher, hugging him tight.

"You know, Christopher, I believe you will make a fine explorer someday. You are already a great voyageur!" said Meggie with a smile on her face.

LeClaire reached out and slapped Chris across the shoulder. "You would make a fine partner with Meggie and me if you decide to stay."

Meggie reached out and hugged Nicholas. "Little Fawn, I will miss you. You are always welcome in my canoe."

"Thanks, Meggie. I'll miss you too," said Nick, and he wished he could take his new friends back home with him.

"Let's get going, Nick!" said Chris. "Hey, do you think Mom and Dad will ground us for life?"

Nick knew his parents would just be happy to have them back home.

Meggie led the way up the beach to the village. There on the street leading to the fort was a small lodge. Outside the lodge stood a man in a long black outfit that looked like a dress with hundreds of tiny buttons down the front. He wore a big brimmed, black hat on his head.

"*Bonjour!*" Meggie called and spoke to the man in French. The priest smiled when he saw Meggie and LeClaire and put out his arms to welcome them.

LeClaire leaned over to the boys and whispered, "Do you see why he is called Black Robe?" The boys smiled at LeClaire as Meggie continued to speak with the priest.

"Madame, she tells the Black Robe of your adventures and your wish to return home," said LeClaire, interpreting for the boys.

"He looks worried to me," Chris remarked. "What if he can't help us?"

LeClaire patted Christopher on the shoulder, "Do not worry."

Meggie soon joined the boys and LeClaire, looking very serious. "The Black Robe, he has never helped anyone with your problem before," said Meggie. "He will help you if he can! We must follow him into the lodge, where he will bless you with water. That is all he can do."

Chris and Nick looked at each other and gulped hard.

"It will be fine," said LeClaire. "We will be there beside you."

The four of them entered the dimly-lit lodge. It was hot inside. Hundreds of tiny candles shimmered in silver holders all around the room, and the sweet smell of incense filled the air. The lodge looked just like the lodges at L'Arbre Croche, except this one had a big silver cross standing on a table.

The Black Robe approached the boys with a small bowl of water in his hand and began singing a song in French. He walked around and around, singing and sprinkling them with the water. Meggie and LeClaire stood in the shadows of the lodge and watched silently.

The heat and the sweet smell of incense started to make Nicholas feel dizzy. It's so hot in here! he thought.

The Black Robe continued walking around and around, singing and sprinkling water.

I don't feel so well, thought Nicholas, as he closed his eyes and breathed deeply. Suddenly, the room began to feel like it was spinning around him. No longer able to stand, Nick lay down on the dirt floor as the Black Robe continued to sprinkle him with water.

Nick couldn't remember how long he lay on the floor, but when he opened his eyes he was no longer in the lodge. He was outside! And Chris was now standing over him, sprinkling water from the red canteen onto his face.

"Nick! Nick! That's it, little brother, open your eyes!"

Nick blinked a couple of times and slowly sat up, wiping his face with his shirt sleeve.

"You OK?" asked Chris. "I thought you'd never wake up."

Nick sat there for a moment trying to remember where he was. "Chris, what happened? Where are Meggie and LeClaire? Where's the Black Robe?"

"Who?" asked Chris.

"Meggie and LeClaire and the Black Robe. You know who I mean, don't you?"

"Wow, little brother, you really got some whack on the head when you fell. There isn't anyone here except us," explained Chris. "I raced to the tree like we planned. When I got there, I found your rock lying on the ground. I thought you beat me to the tree, but when I couldn't find you, I started looking around. Then, I cut back through the woods. And there you were, lying on the ground."

"You found my rock? By the big tree?" asked Nick.

"Yeah, here it is." Chris dug deep into his pocket and pulled out the turtle warrior rock. "There's no mistaking this rock. You know, Nick, I think you're right about this little fellow. He really does look like a turtle warrior, like an Indian turtle warrior." Chris laughed as he handed the rock to Nick.

Nick grabbed his magical rock, remembering the great adventure they had just been on. But how did the rock get to the tree? Nick wondered.

"Chris, what time is it?"

Chris looked down at his watch. "Wow, it's almost time for Mom to be back from the store. We better get going or we will be grounded for life."

Chris helped Nick to his feet and the two boys made their way to the crest of the dune.

"You know that tree of yours, Chris, the big one in the middle of the woods? I think you're right. There must have been something really special that happened there once, a long time ago."

Chris smiled at Nick as they ran down the dune toward the beach and home.